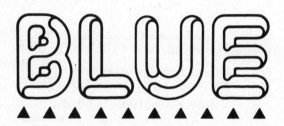

BLUE

▲ ▲ ▲ ▲ ▲ ▲ ▲ ▲ ▲

JAMES HENEGHAN

Cover by
Marc Sorozan

Scholastic Canada Ltd.

Scholastic Canada Ltd.
123 Newkirk Road, Richmond Hill, Ontario, Canada L4C 3G5

Scholastic Inc.
730 Broadway, New York, NY 10003, USA

Ashton Scholastic Limited
Private Bag 1, Penrose, Auckland, New Zealand

Ashton Scholastic Pty Limited
PO Box 579, Gosford, NSW 2250, Australia

Scholastic Publications Ltd.
Villiers House, Clarendon Avenue, Leamington Spa,
Warwickshire, CV32 5PR UK

Canadian Cataloguing in Publication Data

Heneghan, James, 1930-
    Blue

ISBN 0-590-74044-X

I. Title.

PS8565.E54B5 1991   jC813'.54   C91-094309-5
PZ7.H45Bl 1991

8 7 6 5 4 3 2 1   Printed in Canada   1 2 3 4 5 6 7 8/9
                    Manufactured by Gagné Printing

For Ann, Rob, John and Leah.

By the same author:
The Case of the Marmalade Cat

CHAPTER 1

"You killed him!"

The boy's fists clenched. Hot tears brimmed up behind his eyelids as he glared up at the man on the tractor. "You killed him!" he said again.

The yard was all glare and heat under a sky hard as baked enamel, like the paint on the old tractor. The man stepped down off the tractor and dropped the heavy carcass into the boy's trembling arms. The dog's black and white coat was matted with blood.

"There was nothing I could do, boy," the man

growled. "He came a-running at the tractor." He wiped his bloody hands on the back of his blue jeans. "The dog was old."

In the hard brightness of the day, boy and dog were a darker glare brushed into the prairie landscape like a flick of shiny oil paint. The boy lurched away and, hugging the dog to his chest, carried him over to the grove of birches beside the farmhouse. The mother saw the boy through the kitchen window and came hurrying from the house. When she saw that the dog was dead, she dropped to her knees and wrapped her arms about boy and animal.

"He killed him!" the boy choked. He jerked his head back at the man driving away in the old John Deere tractor.

"No, Andy," said his mother, "Mr. McAtee wouldn't harm Patch."

"He did it deliberately," Andy insisted bitterly. "The very first day we came here he told me Patch was too old and useless. He hated Patch."

He knelt and placed the dog down on the grass. Then he fetched a shovel from the toolshed and buried him in the grove of birches near the farmhouse. Over his grave he placed a rusty tractor axle which had the rough shape of a cross.

Dinner was strained. Andy said nothing to McAtee, pretended he didn't exist. If McAtee was upset by this behaviour he never showed it. His face was always the same, calm and unmoving. It was as hard to read as one of those old tombstones in the country graveyard up on the hill, where the brown owl hooted all night long.

Andy's mother offered to get him another dog, any kind he wanted.

Andy didn't want another dog. "Patch isn't a TV that's busted and you just go get a new one," he said. He shot an accusing glare across the dinner table at McAtee.

McAtee met his eye. In a quiet voice he said, "Seems to me your mother is aiming to help you, boy." He pushed back his chair, stood up, and tossed his napkin onto the table. His face was flushed. "Excuse me. I got chores still left to do." He turned and walked out.

Andy's Uncle Ted said, "A good hunting dog is what you need out here, Andy." Uncle Ted was his father's brother. Today he had stayed on to supper, but he lived on his own ten kilometres away in Pendleton and drove his battered old Chevy truck back and forth every day to McAtee's farm. Uncle Ted smiled fondly and patted his nephew on the head and Andy jerked away; he was small for his age and hated it when people patted him on the head.

"I don't need another dog," repeated Andy.

"Hunting dog is useful," said Uncle Ted. "Useful as a jar of whusky to a thirsty man."

"You're the same as Maggoty," said Andy. "Who says everyone has to be *useful?* Why can't things live for themselves? Who says a tree or a dog or a person has got to be useful?" He swung angrily away and started out of the kitchen, which also served as a dining room in the old farmhouse.

His mother called him back sharply. "Andy! There's no call to speak to your uncle like that. Come back here and apologize."

He stopped in angry confusion. His uncle's face wore a hurt expression. "I'm sorry, Uncle Ted," he muttered.

"And you're to stop calling Mr. McAtee by that awful name, do you hear?" said his mother. "It's disrespectful and cruel."

Andy flung himself out the back door and sat on the steps to pull on his workboots. It was time to clean out the hog pens. He too had his useful purpose in life: everything and everyone at Maggoty's Kirriemuir Farm must in some way be useful, he thought as he jerked at the laces of his boots.

His usefulness on McAtee's farm was the hogs. All summer he had been learning how to feed and take care of them. Now, in September, there was also school in Pendleton, and he felt that his usefulness was being stretched to the limit. Today after school there had been the basketball tryouts, and now his arms and legs ached with fatigue. It took him two hours to finish his chores.

He drove the old John Deere tractor into the shed, the same tractor that had killed Patch. It had been a long, heavy, brooding kind of day, the kind that spawns a storm. Andy sank wearily onto the back steps to pull off his muddy boots. He remembered how Patch used to sit on the steps, tail thumping, waiting for him to drive the tractor into the yard and put it away for the night. By the time he was closing the shed doors, Patch would be at his side, grinning all over his face.

He threw his workboots onto the porch and pushed his way through the door. The screen door banged behind him.

"That you, Mr. McAtee?" Andy's mother called from the living room.

"No," he yelled, "it's me." Couldn't she tell?

Maggoty never let the screen door bang shut, he always entered quietly, the way he did everything else: slow, quiet, deliberate.

Maggoty was a good name for Patch's killer, he thought. A giant maggot feasting on death.

His mother came through into the kitchen. "You look tired, Andy. What will it be, milk or a bottle of pop?"

"Pop's fine. I'll get it." He slid one out of the refrigerator and took it to the big table. It was dark ash, like the kitchen cabinets, and covered with a dark blue tablecloth. The kitchen wallpaper was blue, too, but pale like a robin's egg, with a pattern of small white seagulls flying in columns across the walls.

"Mr. McAtee is late. Did you see him on the way in?"

"He's tinkering with one of the diesels," said Andy. "The light was on in the tractor shed."

"Piece of apple pie with your pop?"

"Thanks." His mother put a plate before him.

The faint rattle of the screen door announced McAtee's arrival.

Quinn McAtee was a big man. He wore a red and green checkered shirt and his blue jeans were held up with a wide belt, black and shiny. His eyes and the lock of dark hair that fell on his forehead glistened like his belt. His face was all angles, the cheekbones high and hard and the mouth wide with no sign of softness. When he came through a doorway, he filled it, thick and dark and powerful.

His size and strength reminded Andy of how small he was. According to his mother, however, size wasn't important. "It's what's inside that counts," she always said. But when you were small you had to work twice as hard as everyone else.

"Andy is having apple pie. Would you like some, Mr. McAtee?"

"No thanks, Mrs. Scott." McAtee reached into the refrigerator for a bottle of beer, unscrewed the cap, dropped it into the garbage bag under the sink and sat down at the table across from Andy. The bottle of beer was lost in his huge fist.

"Swine all right, boy?" he asked in his gruff voice.

Andy nodded his head and gave a grunt, but kept his attention on the pie, not looking up at McAtee. Uncle Ted called them hogs, but swine was the right word, for hogs were pigs weighing over 120 pounds. Andy was proud of his knowledge of them, and proud of the effort he took looking after them. The last thing he wanted was Maggotty thinking he couldn't handle the job; he intended to show him he could work as hard as anyone, even harder.

"I'm asking you a question, boy," said McAtee quietly.

Andy glared at him. "I said yes!"

"Yes, sir," said McAtee even more quietly than before. His dark eyes bored into him.

In the heavy silence that followed, McAtee didn't taken his eyes off Andy. He was waiting, relaxed, his arm stretched out on the table, the beer bottle in his fist.

Andy shot a glance at his mother. She gave him a look which clearly said, "Mind your manners."

He turned to McAtee. "Yes, *sir!*" he said. He pushed away his unfinished pie and jumped to his feet. The legs of the chair made a loud scraping rattle on the linoleum floor. He jerked open the cupboard door underneath the sink and dropped the pop bottle in with the empties with a loud clatter. Then he scraped the remains of his pie into the garbage, rinsed the plate and tossed it into the dishrack. He shot his mother a dark look and marched into the living room, then threw himself onto the couch where he sat tight, arms folded, fists clenched, listening to the silence crackling in the other room and hating McAtee with a pure and burning hatred.

"Looks like a storm heading this way," said Andy's mother, breaking the silence.

McAtee gave a grunt.

His mother came into the living room. "Will it hold up the harvesting?" she said to McAtee over her shoulder as he followed her in.

McAtee scowled at her. Then he gave a shrug of his big shoulders. "Maybe, maybe not." He sat in his easy chair beside the fireplace, the bottle still in his fist. Andy lurched to his feet and made for the stairs.

"You off to bed, Andy?" said his mother.

"Soon as I shower," he said.

"How was your basketball tryout? You didn't say. Did you make the team?"

He paused on the stairs. McAtee was watching him with those big, burning, dark eyes of his. "I won't know until tomorrow."

His mother looked up at him, happy. "I know you'll make it. How could Pendleton High manage without Andy Scott on their team, I'd like to know!" She turned to McAtee. "Andy misses his friends, but he's sure to make new ones on the team."

McAtee took a swig of his beer but said nothing.

"Goodnight, Mom." He turned to go, but McAtee's quiet voice stopped him. "Andy."

Andy looked down at him, surprised at hearing his name in McAtee's mouth — he was usually *boy*.

"Basketball is fine," said McAtee, "so long as it don't interfere with your work here. Looking after the swine is your number one priority, OK?"

Andy's mother said, "But, Mr. McAtee, team practices end late. School is a priority too, don't you think?" Her voice was so low and gentle that Andy had to strain to hear it.

"Basketball isn't school, basketball is play," said McAtee softly. "Work comes first. If the boy can't handle the job, then I'll be forced to hire someone else."

Andy's mother said, "Yes, but . . . "

McAtee gave the arm of his chair a gentle tap with the heel of his beer bottle. "Mrs. Scott, if the boy is to do the work and take the responsibility, then he's big enough to speak for himself." He waited, looking up at Andy on the stairs.

"I can speak for myself." He didn't try to hide the contempt in his voice. "I can handle the job all right,

Mr. McAtee. I don't expect I'll be picked for the team, but if I am, I'll do my work, don't you worry." Then he added with bitter triumph in his voice, "Nothing has got in the way of the work so far, has it?"

McAtee's head jerked as though Andy had struck him. For a moment his dark eyes burned with a fierce fire, then he dropped his head and stared at the floor. "I got no complaints," he said quietly.

Later, in his room, Andy thrust dark thoughts of McAtee from his mind as he hurried through his math homework. Then he started on his reading assignment for English, a science fiction story about a flying saucer. But his attention kept wandering and he soon gave it up. Black thoughts of McAtee rushed back and filled his mind: Maggoty the murderer of dogs; Maggoty the slavedriver of Kirriemuir Farm.

He hurled his English reader across the room.

If Miss Oliver gave a quiz, he'd fail it, that's all. Besides, who could get interested in a load of hog manure about flying saucers when there were so many important things on his mind — like making the basketball team, for one. He'd played his hardest, but Coach Taylor was like McAtee:

you could never tell what he was thinking. He knew he was too small for a basketball player, but he also knew he was fast. When he'd applied for a place, Coach Taylor had looked him up and down. "Why don't you try for soccer, kid?" he'd said. Some of the other kids sniggered behind his back. The coach gave them a hard look and they shuffled their feet. "I don't want to play soccer," Andy had answered, "I'm a good basketball player." "We'll see," was all Coach Taylor had said. Later, after the tryout with sweat running into his eyes, he had looked over at the coach but had been able to read nothing in his face.

Andy slid off his bed and retrieved his English reader from the floor. He examined it. It wasn't damaged. He'd have to do better in controlling that temper of his. He dropped the book back into his schoolbag and threw himself onto the bed. He looked around his bedroom, at the pale yellow wallpaper with a pattern of white and yellow corncobs, which the sun in the mornings accentuated to a warm, egg-yolk brightness. On his bed was a brown and orange quilt. The hardwood floor had on it two brown rugs, one at the foot of the bed and the other at the side. There was an ancient pine chest of drawers for his clothes and a pine desk and chair over in the corner near the dormer window. It was a good room.

The storm moved in and rattled the windows, and he lay in bed, overtired but awake, listening to the howl of the wind and staring out the window at the wild swing of the birches. The two trees nearest the house writhed back and forth, tossing their heads at one another in the high wind. It was a long time before he managed to fall asleep, and when he finally did, he dreamed that it was Patch's spirit that cried and howled through the birches where he was buried, making the tall trees struggle in lunatic frenzy like wild tortured animals.

CHAPTER 2

The screech of the wind woke him up. He pulled the covers up over his ears. He was afraid of storms. And cockroaches. And heights. Especially heights.

Andy peeped at the digital clock radio beside his bed; it glowed a red 2:10. He tried going back to sleep but the wind and the distant thunder scared him. He lay in the darkness staring out the window, waiting for the wind to blow the tossing birches down on to the house, as it surely must. He tried to still his fears by thinking about what his mother had said about making new friends. But he didn't want new friends; he wanted his old ones back. Morgie Wilks had been his best friend; they had lived on the same block for years. Morgie had never been afraid of storms. Morgie was scared of nothing. He was the most unscared guy Andy had ever met. Andy would never admit to Morgie that storms scared him. Not that Morgie would ever laugh, but Andy kept his fears to himself.

And he missed Patch. The loss of his childhood pet was an emptiness inside him.

There were other things he missed too; life here at Kirriemuir was so different from life in the city.

One thing he did not miss, however, was their old apartment. It was hard to believe that a mere three months ago it had been just the three of them — Andy, his mother, and Patch — living in that run-down, third-floor, third-rate apartment with its noisy plumbing and its cockroaches. Whenever his mother attacked the dark corners with a can of roach spray, their numbers seemed to increase. In the winter months, when his mother was working late and he came into a dark apartment, he used to pause outside the door and take off his shoes. Then he would open the door

quietly, switch on the light, and hunt cockroaches. He would throw himself in and pounce
on the scurrying black creatures of darkness with
fear and hatred, crushing them with shoes pounding like hammers. He killed the big ones first
before they could disappear into the cracks in the
floor and under the skirting board and between
the broken plaster of the walls. The brown babies
he then killed at his leisure, for they were slower
and not as afraid of the light. When he had killed
as many of the enemy as he could, he made a body
count. On a good night he could kill as many as
fifteen, not counting the babies.

How do cockroaches find their way around in
the dark? he used to wonder. Do they have special
eyes, or do those obscenely long waving antennae
stroke the black shape of the night? Often he
dreamed of cockroaches scrabbling all over him
when he was asleep in bed in the darkness and he
would wake in a cold sweat, brushing the dream
out of his ears and eyes with frantic fingers.

Andy's mother wouldn't miss their old apartment, or the city: he was sure of that. Five years
as a waitress in the Lemon Tree Bar and Grill,
depending on tips to augment her tiny salary, had
been turning her into a dull-eyed drudge.

So when Ted Scott, Andy's uncle, wrote that the farmer he worked for, Quinn McAtee, needed a housekeeper, his mother had seized the opportunity. Kirriemuir would mean a roof over their heads and food in their bellies, she said. They wouldn't have to worry any more about scraping together the money for the rent and the heat and the phone. It was a chance to escape the deadly grind of poverty.

So she gave the Lemon Tree Bar and Grill a week's notice, sold their old couch and kitchen set to Mrs. Horlacher on the second floor, and packed their few things in the ancient Pontiac. Then they set out to begin a new life in the clear, unpolluted air of Kirriemuir.

Morgie had skipped school to see him off. "Wish I was coming with you, Andy," he had said seriously. Andy hadn't known what to say in reply, for Morgie was seldom serious about anything: mocking yes, serious no. Morgie's freckled earnestness had taken him by surprise. When he recovered he said, "I wish you were coming too. I'll miss you Morgie, more than anything." And Morgie had lowered his head and kicked the curb with his worn-out sneakers.

So they left the city. After two days of dusty

driving they arrived at Kirriemuir Farm. A red sun was just about to disappear over the prairie horizon and the harmonious clash of sunset sounds — the bark of a dog, the lowing of cattle, the grunting of hogs, and the clatter of chickens — combined to fall on the evening air like a chorus of welcome.

Ted Scott was in the yard to take his sister-in-law's hands in his own and kiss her gallantly on the cheek. "Lucy, you haven't changed a bit. Almost forgot what a fine lookin' woman you are." He stood back a pace, his hands on her shoulders and his eyes twinkling. The tone of his voice was playful. "Bit thin, maybe. Need fattening up. Well, you came to the right place." He laughed.

Andy's mother studied her brother-in-law carefully. "Good to see you, Ted, after all this time." She smiled.

There was something in her words, Andy couldn't say what, something cautious, as though she were holding back from a question or a judgement.

Uncle Ted shook Andy gravely by the hand. This was the first time he had ever met his uncle. He looked like all the pictures Andy had ever seen of his father, except that Uncle Ted had a vague, almost foolish air about him. He was tall and thin, with a sharp pointed nose that he pulled on occasionally after he'd spoken. Andy supposed that years and years of pulling had made it into its present shape. Andy liked him; he seemed gentle and friendly, and his eyes twinkled with good humour.

"Mr. McAtee is in the tractor shed," said Uncle Ted. He led them away from the dusty Pontiac. Patch, confused by all the new smells, followed behind.

McAtee was bent over a tractor, a wrench in his big fist, and when he straightened up he was looking down at them with dark eyes in a face burned and crinkled by the sun. His shoulders were wide and powerful and his arms and neck were tanned the colour of molasses.

"Mr. McAtee," said Uncle Ted, "this is my sister-in-law Lucy Scott, and her boy Andy."

McAtee still held the wrench in his oily hand. He gave a nod at Andy's mother and let his eyes flicker quickly over Andy. "I hope you understand that the work here is hard, Mrs. Scott. As well as the housework and the cooking there's the chickens to take care of and the vegetable garden out back." He paused, as if awaiting a reply, and when she smiled happily and made none, he allowed his dark eyes to fall on Andy again. "As for the boy, his uncle will teach him how to take care of the swine." His voice was deep and gruff.

Andy's mother said, "Mr. McAtee, Andy is still a child."

"Work and discipline are good for a boy, Mrs. Scott," said McAtee as though Andy were not there. "On a farm, everyone does useful work. The boy will tend the swine and help you in the garden."

She was about to say something else, but Andy interrupted. "That's all right, Mom, I can work as hard as anybody. I'll do my share."

McAtee grunted. "Take them up to the house, Ted, and show them where everything is."

Andy looked around for Patch. He had wandered off. "Patch!" he called. An answering bark came from the rear of the shed. Patch was busy investigating the dog whose bark they had heard when they drove into the yard. It was a long-haired collie, sable and white, the sable almost as dark as McAtee's sunburned arms. A rope was tied through its collar to the axle of a second tractor at the back of the shed. Andy ran his fingers through the collie's thick coat by way of a greeting. Then he went back to the tractor where McAtee was working. His mother had gone up to the house with Uncle Ted.

"Mr. McAtee," said Andy, "why is your dog tied up?"

McAtee didn't stop working. He spoke over his shoulder. "Dog's always tied up when she ain't working. A working dog ain't a pet. So you don't go petting her, boy, you understand?"

"What's her name?"

"Got no name. She's just a dog."

"Every dog has to have a name, even a working dog."

McAtee's answer was a grunt as he pulled hard on the wrench.

"What kind of work does she do?" said Andy.

"Drover work."

"What's drover work?"

"Herds cattle into the pens. Or down the road to market. Swine too, sometimes. And she finds the ones that get themselves lost."

Andy liked that idea. "She's a finder. That's what I'll call her, Finder."

"I'd like it better if you and your mongrel . . . "

"His name's Patch, and he's not a mongrel, he's a purebred mixture of terrier and bison."

McAtee turned and stared at him.

Andy grinned. "That's my mother's joke, not mine."

"All the same, he's a city dog," said McAtee. "Looks too old to be of much use. City dogs don't take to living on a farm."

"Patch likes it here, I can tell," said Andy. "And he likes Finder."

"Stay away from the collie. I told you she ain't for petting and spoiling. Leave her be. You hear me, boy?"

"Yes, sir."

Later, he told his mother about the dog that had no name. "She finds things that are lost, so I named her Finder."

"Then she'll be a mighty busy dog," his mother said with a smile. "People lose many things."

Now, as he huddled under the covers watching the storm through his bedroom window blow closer to the farmhouse, he felt as if those first days on the farm had happened a long, long time ago, to a boy much younger than himself. He pulled the covers up over his ears and closed his eyes, but a thumping sound from out in the yard wouldn't let him sleep. He pushed himself out of bed, padded over to the window, and looked down at the yard. The hard, steady thumping sound punctuated the driving rain.

Somebody was standing out in the storm over near the tractor shed, splitting logs for kindling. The axe rose and fell with a slow, measured ferocity. A double flash of lightning revealed Mc-Atee, stripped to the waist, the rain lashing his body. His face was wet and dark and intense and the muscles of his arms and shoulders appeared swollen with a terrible strength.

Andy stood at the window for several minutes watching the man he had learned to hate, and then he crawled back under the covers.

Amid the sounds of the wind and the rain and the falling axe blade, he finally fell asleep.

CHAPTER 3

This time he slept for only a couple of hours. It was the crash of the thunder over his head that woke him. Wind and rain lashed the house. Lightning split the night in two.

He stared wide-eyed at the window. He had been dreaming about a flying saucer. That stupid English assignment! The flying saucer had flown out of his stormy dream to crash-land in the yard near the tractor shed. Its alien pilot, trapped in the saucer, had been bleeding to death. What a dream!

He tried to remember the rest of it, but couldn't. All he knew was that he had felt a tremendous urgency to save the pilot, which was when the thunder had jerked him awake.

Lightning lit up the room, and was followed immediately by an explosive boom of thunder.

He slipped out of bed and pressed his nose against the cold window. He remembered McAtee with his axe, but McAtee was gone. Storms on the prairie are painted on a wider canvas than those in the city: the whole bowl of the sky lit up, and thunder rolled across the empty land in booming waves.

Outside the window, wind and rain lashed the barn and the sheds and the yard. The grove of birches tossed and twisted in nightmare shapes. Over the crash of the storm Andy thought he could hear the barking of a dog. It had to be Finder. He peered out into the darkness, his nose still pressed up against the glass. Something was moving beyond the tractor shed.

It was a dog. But not a collie, not Finder. Besides, Finder would be tied up for the night in the barn or one of the sheds. Andy opened the window, pushing it out against the force of the storm. The rain lashed his face and the wind screeched around the house. Now he could see that the dog was running frantically around a strange object that looked like . . .

He stared in disbelief.

Like a flying saucer!

But not really a flying saucer. More like a flying golfball. It was about the size of Andy's tractor, the one he used to take care of the hogs, but the golfball was perfectly spherical. It was one of those Air Force experimental aircraft, he decided. He turned from the bedroom window and raced down the stairs.

He was shrugging himself into his rain slicker at the back door, when he heard his mother hurrying down the stairs behind him. "Andy!" she called.

Then McAtee's voice. "What is it?" Cool, commanding.

"An aircraft crashed in the yard!" yelled Andy.

"Wait here, boy. Stay with your mother." He pulled on an army issue rainslicker over his robe and ran out into the lashing rain. A flash of lightning illuminated his broad back.

Andy and his mother stood in the open doorway, watching. The dog barked. McAtee was suddenly back, his wet face glistening in the light from the kitchen, and Andy was reminded of the axe swinging fiercely in the storm. "Mrs. Scott — phone for an ambulance!" McAtee yelled over the noise of the storm. He turned to Andy. "Bring the flashlight from the cupboard over the stove, then come lend a hand."

Andy grabbed the flashlight — he had to stand on a chair to get to the cupboard — and followed McAtee out to the aircraft. The flashlight revealed that the giant golfball was transparent. It had broken almost in two with the force of the impact. Andy could see the still shape of the pilot strapped into his seat in the centre of the craft, which, though pockmarked like a golfball, now looked more like a glass bubble.

"Shine the light over here!" yelled McAtee as he reached into the shattered wreck. He tore away the seatbelt and lifted the pilot carefully on to the ground as though he weighed nothing.

Andy had forgotten about the dog. Now it came nosing and whimpering at the pilot.

McAtee's backhand swipe hurled the dog back out of the way.

The dog whined. Andy thought it looked like an old English sheepdog, though it was hard to tell because of the rain and darkness. He ran his fingers through the soaked fur of the animal's ruff. No collar. "Take it easy, buddy," he said. The dog whined again and Andy suddenly thought about a man. Except it wasn't a thought, it was more like a picture in his head. Nor was it a man; it was more like a doll, a doll with a small, heart-shaped face and huge liquid eyes. He shook his head. The picture went away. The dog was quiet. Andy turned to help McAtee.

"Shine the light," McAtee shouted.

As Andy shone the light he noticed something he'd missed earlier: the pilot's left leg had been sheared off just below the knee, and the floor of the cabin was soaked in blood. "Is he dead?"

McAtee didn't answer. Instead, he quickly tore off one of his pajama legs and tied it around the pilot's amputated leg to stem the flow of blood. Then he unstrapped and removed the pilot's helmet.

Andy moved closer with the flashlight. He saw the man's face: the eyes were wide open, glazed, dying. The face was small and heart-shaped, like a doll's, and the huge liquid eyes seemed to fill most of it.

When McAtee saw the face, he stepped backward in alarm. "What the — "

The rain pounded down. Wind shrieked

through the birches and under the eaves of the house.

"Is there anything I can do?" It was Andy's mother with a plastic cape over her shoulders. She wore no hat; the rain plastered her long dark hair to her head.

"No, nothing," said McAtee, "except maybe you better call the police to come out and take a look." When she saw the pilot's face her hand went to her mouth and she gave a cry.

"Call the police, Mrs. Scott," said McAtee calmly.

She hurried back to the house just as the ambulance drove into the yard.

Andy waved the flashlight. The ambulance had come from Pendleton. It had been quick. Two men jumped out and bent over the pilot. They looked at one another. Then they looked at the shattered aircraft. Finally they looked at Andy and McAtee. "What is this?" asked the driver, a big man with a flat, fleshy nose. "Some kind of Hallowe'en trick?"

"It's no trick," growled McAtee. "Why don't you two do your job instead of standing around asking fool questions!"

"He's dead," said the second ambulance man.

"Bled to death, by the looks of it."

The dog barked.

The ambulance men lifted the body onto a stretcher and loaded it into the back of the ambulance.

The man and the boy stood in the rain. The lightning flashed and the thunder cracked. They watched the rear lights of the ambulance as it drove out of the yard towards the road.

The dog followed the ambulance, bounding along silently behind its rear wheels.

As Andy followed McAtee back to the house he couldn't stop thinking about how he had seen the pilot's alien face in his mind *before* McAtee removed the helmet, *before* he knew what the pilot looked like.

And he remembered the dream that had jerked him awake so abruptly: the strange aircraft in his dream was exactly like the one that now lay broken and shattered in the yard of Kirriemuir Farm.

CHAPTER 4

A policeman from the town came and went. He was followed by a pair of eager plain-clothes detectives who drove up in an unmarked car, inspected the strange aircraft, asked a lot of questions, and then tore off in a great hurry.

The storm blew itself out by six o'clock. Andy's mother talked about going back to bed but nobody moved. At seven o'clock, three limousines and a military truck pulled into the yard. Out of the truck poured a dozen soldiers with helmets and rifles. They immediately formed a tight circle around the aircraft and stood facing outward, rifles at the ready. A second army of men in identical, smart business suits climbed out of the limousines and inspected the aircraft and took pictures. Then they came into the house, introduced themselves as special investigation agents, used the telephone, took more pictures, and asked more questions.

McAtee left the talking to Andy's mother and stood quietly, his dark eyes watching her face as she patiently told their story for the umpteenth time.

"Did the pilot communicate to you in any way?" asked the chief questioner, a thin man with a face like an axe blade, who had introduced himself simply as "Frost."

"He was dead," said Andy's mother.

They were sitting in the kitchen. The thin man remained standing. Sometimes he walked about, picking up and examining small objects in the kitchen as if he hoped to find the answers to his questions in them. Most of the men had gone back outside to walk around the aircraft and take measurements and more pictures.

"Did the pilot give you anything?"

"No."

"Nothing? Are you sure?"

"He was dead."

"Did he say anything?"

"You're not listening, mister," growled McAtee, "we already told you he was dead."

"Did you take anything off the pilot's body or remove anything from the aircraft?"

There seemed no end to the questions.

A second military truck arrived pulling a low-loader trailer behind it. They loaded the aircraft onto the trailer and left. Two of the limousines also left, taking most of the investigators.

The thin man said, "Mr. and Mrs. McAtee, this aircraft and its pilot are classified top secret. We are not saying that this is a confirmed alien encounter. We are saying nothing at this point. And you three people are to say nothing. You will impress this upon the boy. Your country demands your co-operation. The strictest secrecy must be observed. Not a word, not a sign. The slightest leak on your part could constitute a breach of the official security regulations. Do you all understand?"

"There's something *you* don't understand, mister," said McAtee. "This lady is Mrs. Scott, my housekeeper. She works here. And if you've finished, I've a mind to see some *useful* work done before the day is wasted entirely."

The thin man stopped his pacing about and took a long look at McAtee as though he too might be an alien. "We've finished for now, Mr. McAtee, but there may be more questions at a later time. You are not to leave this area without clearance. I can be contacted at this number." He handed McAtee a card, but McAtee ignored the outstretched hand and made no move to take the card. Frost placed the card on the table.

Andy was in agony wondering whether to say anything about his strange dream or about the image of the pilot that had flashed in his head before he saw his face. But Frost asked him no questions and he said nothing; they would only laugh at him or ask a million more questions he couldn't answer.

Nobody mentioned the dog.

When the men had all gone, Andy and his mother and McAtee sat in the kitchen drinking coffee. They were tired and bewildered. "An alien from outer space!" Andy's mother whispered, staring into her coffee cup.

McAtee said nothing. He watched Andy's mother, frowning as though it was not the alien from outer space that bothered him but Lucy Scott herself.

Andy said, "Just before it crashed in the yard I dreamt about it." He waited for a response. Nothing. They weren't listening. His mother and McAtee were staring at each other, not saying anything. To Andy, they looked funny sitting there like that, not saying anything, just looking at one another over the tops of their coffee cups.

He said it again. "I had this dream. . . . "

"You look tired, Mrs. Scott," said McAtee.

"The excitement . . . " She smiled wearily.

"Go lie down for a few hours," said McAtee. He stared at her, his dark eyes burning. She stared back at him, her eyes the colour of Chinese jade. It was if they had forgotten Andy was there. He could see in his mother's eyes the tiny flecks of orange that sometimes caught the sun and glinted like gold.

"What did you say about a dream?" his mother said at last, taking her eyes from McAtee's face.

"I dreamed about the alien crashing in the yard just before it actually happened."

His mother said, "Seems to me I was having a dream about flying too." She bit her lip, trying to recall the dream. She shook her head. "It's gone.

I can't remember."

"Did you have a dream, Mr. McAtee?" It was the first time Andy had addressed him voluntarily since Patch's death, but the master of Kirriemuir wasn't listening; his mind was somewhere else. Andy said to his mother, "You ask him."

"Mr. McAtee," she said gently, "Andy is talking to you."

McAtee's eyes looked puzzled.

"He wants to know if you were having a dream just before the . . . thing . . . crashed in the yard."

McAtee turned to Andy. "If I was, I don't recall."

"When you saw the alien's face. Were you surprised? I mean, had you seen the face before?"

"What you getting at, boy? Of course I never saw anything like it before."

Andy studied McAtee's face. He knew nothing. "What about you, Mom?"

"Never," she said. "It wasn't a frightening face, though it did give me a shock. It was kind of nice . . . those big eyes. Reminded me of one of those cute loris monkeys you see in a zoo. Big eyes, soft like rain." She glanced at the wall clock over the refrigerator. "You've missed the school bus, Andy. Looks like a day off for you."

Today was the day Coach Taylor would be posting the basketball team. "I'll try to hitch a ride."

His mother said, "I'll make you some breakfast, then I'll drive you in."

"I'd better find Ted and go see how much damage there is in the cornfield," growled McAtee.

They watched him head straight to the tractor shed, kicking aside broken branches and splashing through puddles. Andy said, accusing, "He's been looking at you."

"The yard's a mess."

"He killed Patch. He's cruel."

"He was driving the small tractor, Andy, the one you always drive. Patch knew that. He barked and ran at Mr. McAtee because he was on your tractor."

"I don't care. I hate him."

"He's not like other men, Andy. He was in Vietnam. War changes people. He has lived a very different life. You've got to give him a chance."

Andy gave a sniff. "He always calls me *boy*, like I don't have a name. Like Finder. Kids and dogs are all the same to him."

"He likes you, Andy. He's been alone a long time. He doesn't understand children." She put her arm around his shoulders.

The telephone rang. Andy's mother answered it. He started to take things out of the refrigerator for breakfast. A dog barked outside the back door. "Oh, no!" Andy groaned. He pushed the screen door open. It was the same dog all right, its shaggy coat now dry.

"What you want, dog? You lose your sheep someplace?"

"Who is it, Andy?" called his mother.

"It's that dog again."

She came to the door. "This one looks like a cross between a llama and a dirty mop. Poor thing, he's hungry. Bring him in, there's still a few cans left of Pat—" She stopped, avoiding her son's eyes. "I'll start breakfast if you open up a can of chow for your friend. That was Peggy Matheson on the phone. She's going into Pendleton and will pick you up on the road in about half an hour."

Andy filled Patch's bowl with water and opened a can of Mongrel Meal, Patch's favourite.

The sheepdog gobbled it all up.

Andy and his mother ate their breakfast. "Who do you suppose he belongs to?" said his mother.

Andy shrugged.

"If he's a stray maybe you could keep him."

"I don't want him."

"He looks like a woolly mammoth. He's cute. All those curls — they're really more blue than grey. That would be a good name for him. You could call him Blue."

"I don't want a dog." Andy pushed his chair back and got up from the table. "I especially don't want any dog who's dumb enough to get himself lost." He grabbed his school books. The dog followed him out. "Go get lost someplace else!" he yelled at it.

The dog sat and watched Andy's back as he zig-zagged around the puddles in the long driveway that led to the road. He waited for Mrs. Matheson. There was so much on his mind — the flying golfball, the alien, the dead alien's face, the dream, and finally this funny business between his mother and Maggoty. Maybe he ought to consider skipping school today. How would he ever be able to get through the day keeping it all to himself? Maybe, too, it was a good thing he didn't have any close friends at Pendleton: if Morgie were there he knew, just knew, he'd have to tell him, for he'd always told Morgie everything — well practically everything.

The sun was warm already on the back of his neck. It was going to be a hot day. The fields would dry out pretty fast.

"Wuff." It was the dog sitting beside him.

"I told you to get lost!" growled Andy in a fair imitation of McAtee. "I don't want you."

The dog cocked its head at him and continued to sit.

Mrs. Matheson pulled up in her Ford station wagon. "Jump in, Andy."

He opened the front door and climbed in. The dog tried to follow him. He pushed it out.

"What a fine dog," said Mrs. Matheson, "and what an unusual colour. Your mother forgot to mention you had another dog. What's his name?"

"He's got no name and he's not mine. He's a stray." Andy slammed the door shut.

The dog sat on the side of the road watching the car drive off.

CHAPTER 5

The ride home from Pendleton to Kirriemuir on the school bus took over half an hour, for it stopped often to let people off. Andy asked if anyone on the bus had lost a dog.

"What kind of a dog?" somebody asked.

"A sheepdog. Sort of a blue colour."

"Blue!" somebody else yelled. "Hey, Marty, didn't you lose a blue sheepdog? Or was it a purple poodle?" His laugh was a machine-gun rattle.

"Wrong dog!" Marty screamed back. "The one I lost was a yellow ratcatcher."

Andy concluded that nobody had lost a dog.

He had said nothing all day to anyone about the visitor from outer space, not a word. Keeping the secret had been easy. Those men from the government didn't scare him, but his mother would have been disappointed in him if he'd let it out. And McAtee would think him a blabber, not that he cared what old Maggoty thought anyway. Besides, who at school would ever believe such a story? A golfball from outer space and a dead alien with eyes like eggplants! They would laugh at him.

And there had been other things for Andy to think about. As soon as he got to school he had hurried over to the gym bulletin board. The list of the successful athletes was pinned up for all to see. There was no Andy Scott on the list. He hadn't made the team. His heart bottomed out. It was on account of his size, he knew it. He was too small; the other kids outreached him. All that fast footwork and passing hadn't impressed Coach Taylor one bit.

Cliff Anderson, a kid in his science class, had stopped him during the lunch hour to tell him he was sorry he hadn't made it. "I thought you were in for sure," he said.

"You watched the tryouts?" said Andy.

"My brother is Mark Anderson. You know, the one with the red hair and big mouth?"

Andy had laughed. He knew Mark: he was the joker in the pack. "I see that he made it all right."

"Probably talked the coach into it," said Cliff.

As the bus came over the brow of the hill, Andy could see Kirriemuir down in the valley. Because it was so tall, the silo was always the first thing he saw. It pointed to the enamel blue sky like a slim space rocket. Then after a while he could see the distant barn and sheds huddled together like Monopoly pieces about the farmhouse, and on the far side, the grove of birches and the L-shaped rows of pine trees that served as a windbreak for the house.

The white frame house crouched into itself from the prairie heat under a low red roof, and the two dormer windows appeared from this distance like a pair of tiny watchful eyes looking out over McAtee's rolling fields.

The silo was bigger now, and more like a long blue finger pointing up to the heavens. It was only when you were standing right next to it that the silo ever looked like what it really was — a giant storage bin for the animal feed. Andy remembered staring up at its top when he had first come to the farm and had thought about his dreadful fear of heights. He had glanced fearfully at the thirty-metre ladder which marched up the side of the blue tower.

"You better stay away from her," McAtee had growled at him. "Ladder's got safety hoops all the way up, but that don't mean you couldn't slip and break your neck." He could still feel the awful lurch he'd felt in his belly at the thought of climbing that ladder. "You hear me, boy?" McAtee had growled. "I hear you," Andy had whispered, turning away, his face white with fear.

The door of the bus clattered open. It was his stop. He grabbed his books and stepped off.

The dog was waiting for him.

He ignored it. If he pretended it wasn't there, it would eventually give up and go away. It followed behind him. It was unlikely that the dog had waited there by the side of the road all day. So how come it was waiting for the school bus? Strange dog. Strange colour for a strange dog, blue. He squinted back at the dog without turning his head. Not bright blue like the sky or blue like cornflowers, but darker, more of a violet blue.

He let the screen door slam behind him. The dog

leaped back out of the way. While Andy made himself a peanut butter sandwich the dog sat outside, watching him through the screen door, its tail between its legs. His mother was out, probably in the chicken house. McAtee would be in the cornfield. The sandwich would keep him going until suppertime, until he'd taken care of the swine, all two hundred and fifty of them.

He changed into his workclothes — jeans torn in the right knee and left thigh, white cotton T-shirt with *Tobin & Yates, Seed Merchants* on the front, John Deere tractor cap, and white sport socks. He poured himself a glass of milk, then sat on the back steps to pull on his heavy leather workboots. The afternoon was hot and brassy and hard again as though there'd been no storm at all. The dog sat watching him, its tongue lolling out.

Four times a week Andy had to grind corn in a mixer-mill machine powered by the tractor. That was to be his first job this afternoon. He finished lacing his boots. He didn't look at the dog. If he gave it any encouragement he'd never be rid of it. Feeding it had been a mistake. No more food for lost dogs. It would get the message eventually. The dog was a loser. All wool and nose and nothing much else. Patch, now there had been a real dog. Even in the city with its maze of streets and confusion of sounds and smells, not once had Patch ever got himself lost.

He hooked up the tractor and started the corn mill. While he worked, thoughts of the alien and the flying golfball came to his mind. And the dog.

Why did he suddenly think of the dog? The dog had nosed around the alien's body. It was funny how the dog had turned up at the same time as the flying golfball.

While the corn was grinding, he hauled heavy pails of protein supplement that made his arms ache and tipped them into the hopper to mix with the powdered corn. The dog followed him back and forth with the pails. The mill was noisy and dusty. By the time he was finished, his clothes were full of corn dust. The dog's coat, too, was covered. Now he looked like a giant woolly moth. Andy continued to ignore him.

The next job was to haul the ground corn to the swine, dump it in their feed bins, and fill their troughs with water from the hose. The swine lived in barns with fenced yards. The dog watched the swine feeding.

Andy drove the tractor back to the mill for his next job, a load of unground corn for the sows down in the fenced pasture. The dog followed.

McAtee was in the yard with Finder. The collie's tail wagged enthusiastically when she saw the stray dog. The two dogs began to sniff at each other. McAtee gave a whistle. Finder ran to sit obediently at his heels. The stray dog tried to follow but McAtee waved it away. The dog came back to Andy and sat watching him load the unground corn onto the trailer.

"You aim to keep that stray animal?" McAtee yelled at Andy across the yard.

Andy straightened up. "Dog's no use to me, Mr. McAtee," he yelled back sarcastically, "No sense keeping a dog that has no use, now, is there?" He grinned at the angry expression on Maggoty's face. That would give the high-and-mighty master of Kirriemuir something to think about! What would he do now? Have the useless dog plowed under for fertilizer? Andy chuckled to himself as he watched Maggoty march off, Finder at his heel. He turned back to loading the corn, the smile still on his face. Putting one over on Maggoty felt so good that it almost erased the disappointment of not making the school team.

"Stand away from that dog!"

It was McAtee back. He had a shotgun under

his arm.

Andy glared at him. "What do you plan to do, shoot it?"

The dog sat watching them both.

"Dog that don't belong to nobody is a stray," said McAtee. "I could call the dog pound at Pendleton come take the critter away and have him put down, or I could save the taxpayers the expense and do the job myself."

He stood waiting.

Over in the birches, a red-winged blackbird called to its mate.

McAtee pushed two cartridges into the gun and snapped it closed.

Andy's mother came hurrying from the house. "What is it? What's the matter?"

"I'll ask you to stay out of this, if you don't mind, Mrs. Scott," said McAtee quietly. He raised the gun and pointed it at the dog.

"Don't!" yelled Andy as he threw himself in front of the dog.

Andy's mother screamed and ran to her son.

McAtee lowered the gun. "The dog's yours, boy. You save a life, you're responsible for that life, long as you live."

The dog licked Andy's face.

McAtee turned and strode back to the barn, the shotgun safely under his arm.

Andy looked at his mother.

"Looks like you just saved yourself a dog, Andy," said Lucy Scott.

CHAPTER 6

The dog seemed to know that some kind of a battle had just been fought over him. He sat even closer to Andy to show his gratitude.

"Maggoty was about to shoot you, you stupid wool-ball!" Andy growled. "Why didn't you run for it?"

The dog cocked his head at him.

"He loves to murder dumb animals, and they don't come much dumber than you!"

"Wuff," said the dog.

Andy turned his back on the animal and finished loading the corn. Was he really stuck with it? Was that true what Maggoty had said about being responsible for it for the rest of its life? Without looking back to see if the dog was following, he drove the tractor and trailer over to the sow pasture.

The dog followed and watched him dump the corn over the fence. The sows grunted and snorted enthusiastically at the sight of the food.

As he worked, Andy's mind was on the dog. He didn't know what it was but there was something about it that bothered him, and he couldn't figure out what it was. He should have let Maggoty shoot it. Where could it have come from? Kirriemuir was so big; the nearest neighbour was two kilometres away. Dogs didn't get themselves lost that easily did they? It was no pup; must be at least a couple of years old, Andy reckoned.

As the sows fed, Andy counted them as he always did.

There was one missing!

He groaned. There was only one reason why a sow would miss a meal: she was giving birth — farrowing, it was called — somewhere in the big pasture.

He had to find her and find her quick. McAtee would be angry.

He drove the tractor back to the yard, jumped into the pickup truck, and drove back to the pasture to search for the missing sow. The truck was faster than the tractor for a job like this. The dog followed.

After bumping around the pasture for ten minutes, he found the sow hunkered down in a nest of weeds and alfalfa where she had given birth to a litter of eight pigs. The piglets were asleep, pressed up against her warm fat belly.

This was the second time a sow had farrowed like this since Andy had been in charge of the swine. The last time it happened, McAtee had repeated what his Uncle Ted had already told him: "Sows got to farrow in the barn. Next time you see one of 'em ready to farrow, get her out of the pasture quick as you can, boy, you hear?" Uncle Ted had shown him how to hook up the farrowing crate behind the tractor, how to drive the sow into it, and how to transport it to the farrowing pen in the barn. "If she drops her babies in the pasture, the coyotes are sure to get 'em," explained Uncle Ted. "And if the coyotes don't get 'em, the cold nights will. We can protect 'em better in the barn."

And now another sow had farrowed in the pasture. Usually, a few days before delivery a sow became heavy and swollen with milk. He should have noticed the size of her udder, but he hadn't. McAtee would despise him.

He climbed out of the pickup and approached the sow. The sow grunted a warning for him to stay away from her piglets. The dog's ears pricked up. Andy was too upset with himself to sense any danger.

For such a heavy animal, the sow moved very fast.

The next thing Andy knew, the sow was suddenly charging at him, her tiny pig eyes glittering with rage.

He turned quickly and began to run. But the old hayfield was uneven and bumpy. He ran only a few steps, then tripped and fell. The sow, twice his weight, kept coming, its head down, thundering on like a runaway train.

The dog moved. It ran and stood between the boy and the sow, facing the angry sow as though ready to take the full force of the charge himself.

Andy, now on his knees, yelled, "Look out!"

But the dog didn't budge.

Then the strangest thing happened: just when it appeared that the charging sow was about to strike the dog full force, she came to a dead stop as though she had hit the side of the barn and collapsed, squealing in terror. Then she heaved herself madly up and fled from the dog, back to her writhing piglets.

Andy stood up. His heart was pounding. The whole thing had taken only a few seconds. The dog trotted back and sat at his feet. The boy stared down at the dog. The dog hadn't as much as growled, hadn't barked, had just stood there calmly watching the sow about to steamroll over him. It made no sense. What had stopped the sow and caused it to retreat in terror?

Whatever it was, the dog had saved Andy from a severe mauling, had perhaps even saved his life. Only now did he remember his uncle's warning: "A mother sow can be more dangerous than a wild boar, so keep your distance, Andy!" He groaned. He'd done everything wrong. McAtee would think him a fool. He *was* a fool.

He stumbled back to the pickup. He was trembling. The dog followed. Andy leaned on the side of the truck. His legs felt weak. The dog leaped up into the bed of the truck. Boy and dog regarded one another face to face, skin to wool. The boy ran his fingers through the dog's blue coat. "I don't know how you did it, but . . . thanks . . . Blue."

For the first time since he had become a lost dog at Kirriemuir Farm, Blue wagged his tail.

CHAPTER 7

"I wish I knew your real name, woolball," he said to the dog, "but Blue is as good as any, I guess." He climbed in behind the wheel of the pickup. "Let's go get Uncle Ted to help us with this mean old pig, and let's hope we don't run into Maggoty." He started the engine and drove over to the cornfield.

Uncle Ted wasn't there. Maybe he'd quit for the day. But where was McAtee? The combine harvester was floating in its sea of corn like an abandoned ship. The sun had just gone. Soon it would be dark.

Andy drove over to the house, shut off the motor, and started to search for his uncle. As he approached the tractor shed, Blue at his heels, he heard voices raised in anger. He stopped outside the door, listening.

"I said no!" McAtee's growl.

"Wait, now . . ." Uncle Ted's voice was slow and slurred.

"You'll bunk in the barn for tonight," said McAtee.

"I'm well able to drive. A drop of whusky after a dry day never did a man the bit of harm."

"You did no work all day. Any fool can see you've been at that bottle instead."

"A man's entitled to forget his troubles just once in a while, aren't I right?"

"Give me the keys to your truck, and take what's left of the bottle with you to the barn."

"Man's entitled to forget," mumbled Uncle Ted.

"This is the last time, Scott. I've warned you before. If I find you drunk again, you're finished!"

"Aren't we all finished, every last one of us? Take the keys! You're the hard man, McAtee! Maybe a drop of the malt'd be good for your own suffering soul! Seems to me you might have more to forget than meself."

Andy stood back from the door as McAtee came swinging out with a scowl on his face. "What you standing here for, boy?"

"Sow's farrowed in the pasture."

McAtee swung himself up into the truck. "Let's go get the farrowing crate," was all he said.

They hitched the crate up to the small tractor and headed for the pasture. Blue rode up high beside Andy as he drove. By now it was getting dark, but the tractor had spotlights front and back.

"You tell anyone at school anything about that . . . thing last night?" said McAtee.

"I told no one."

"Dog seems to have taken a shine to you."

"His name is Blue."

When they reached the field, McAtee said, "You leave a marker, boy?"

Andy looked out at the dark, anonymous pasture.

Somewhere out there was a sow and her piglets. He hadn't thought to leave a marker. He could have rolled the empty oil drum off the back of the pickup and left it near the sow. Or he could have pushed a tire iron into the soil and hung his John

Deere cap on it. But he hadn't. He couldn't seem to do anything right. He'd messed up on the farrowing sow, he couldn't make the school team, he was a screw-up plain and simple. It would be impossible to find the sow in the dark; the pasture was too big and the tractor was too slow.

"We'd better go fetch the collie," said McAtee.

Andy thought about the sow and her babies and the nest she had made for them in the pasture. A needle in a haystack; McAtee was right, they would have to go back for Finder.

Suddenly Blue jumped down off the tractor, ran ahead, and then waited. Andy threw the tractor in gear and started after him. Blue trotted ahead in the tractor beams.

After only a few minutes the dog stopped. Andy and McAtee peered ahead. "There they are!" said Andy. He could just make out the shape of the sow, white in the tractor's spotlight beam.

Andy turned the tractor and backed the farrowing crate slowly toward the sow and her piglets. He lowered the crate to the ground and jumped off the tractor. McAtee opened the crate's lift gate. The sow was lit now by the tractor's rear spotlight.

"Grab the plywood," said McAtee. The last time

this had happened it had taken Andy, McAtee and Uncle Ted, all holding sheets of plywood in front of them, to force the sow into the crate; it would be more difficult with only the two of them.

"Be careful," said McAtee, "she could be dangerous."

"She already charged me once," said Andy.

"I'll work my way behind her," said McAtee.

But Blue was too quick for him. The dog came up behind the sow and gave a low growl. The sow lumbered to her feet. The dog advanced slowly, threateningly on the sow, staring her down. The sow turned and made for the crate as though she knew that any protest would be useless. She climbed in. Andy dropped the lift gate with a crash. "Got her!" he cried.

McAtee leaned on his sheet of plywood and gave a whistle of astonishment. "Say, that's quite some drover!" He shook his head in disbelief. "Bring the carton from the tractor and we'll gather up these littl'uns before the coyotes get them."

The baby pigs squealed for their mother until they were reunited with her in the farrowing pen. "Take the dog and go on in, son. Tell your mother I'll be right along."

Andy sat on the back step pulling off his boots.

McAtee had called him *son*. Wonders! And he hadn't got mad over the sow. He couldn't figure it out. Maybe he'd worked off all his anger for the week on poor old Uncle Ted. Blue sat beside him. "You did a great job, Blue. McAtee thinks so too." He tried to imitate McAtee's deep growl. "I think maybe you're gonna be worth your keep around here, dog. You're gonna be *useful!*"

Blue gave a sniff.

Suddenly, Andy had a picture in his mind of Blue chewing on a piece of meat. The remarkable thing about the picture was the way it had just snapped into his mind like switching on a TV set.

Then it happened again, but this time it was a picture of Blue drinking water out of the toilet bowl. The picture snapped off as suddenly as it had come.

Andy scratched his head. There was something funny going on here. Was the dog telling him that he was hungry? He stared at Blue. Blue stared back at him and gave his tail a wag. Andy thought furiously. He thought back to the crash of the flying golfball. He remembered his dream pictures of the alien aircraft crashing, and he remembered also the strange picture he'd had of the alien's face a moment or two before he saw the actual face. That was a mystery. Then there was the funny business of the sow retreating from Blue in terror. And tonight, Blue had seemed to know of Andy's distress in the dark pasture and had led the way to the sow's nest.

He looked Blue in the eye. "You're some drover all right," he said suspiciously. "Come on, I'll get your supper."

His mother was in the living room mending a pair of blue jeans. "School OK today?" she asked.

"Sure, Mom, almost bearable."

"Did you mention to anyone . . . "

"No. Do you think they'd believe me if I said, 'Hey, guys, guess what! A flying saucer crashed in our backyard last night during the storm. I went out to ask the pilot what planet he was from, but he was dead.' Do you think I'm crazy!"

"What about the team?"

"The team?"

"Don't play dumb. The basketball team — did you make it?"

Andy shook his head. "No."

His mother smiled sympathetically. "Never mind, there's always next year. Or you could try out for something else, soccer maybe?"

"Mom, are you planning to stay at this crummy McDonald's farm for another year? Because if you are, I'll run away, I swear! Already I'm beginning to grunt like a hog. I hate it, you know that!"

"It's a good home for us, Andy. Sure, the work is hard, but it's hard everywhere. We need this place and you know it. I love it here and you'll love it too when you decide to give it a chance."

"It wouldn't be so bad if it wasn't for McAtee. You saw him itching to shoot Blue. He's crazy."

Blue lay on the floor, his eyes closed. Andy's mother reached down and ruffled his ears. "Blue is a perfect name for him." She looked up, her face serious. "Andy, I know Mr. McAtee, and I know that he had no intention of shooting the dog. He did it for *you*."

"Huh?" Andy stared at her.

"He made you make up your mind to keep the dog, didn't he?"

"And what if I hadn't done anything? He would have murdered him just as he murdered Patch."

His mother sighed.

"He would have shot him," said Andy, "I know it. You don't see him the way I see him — the way he really is."

"Andy, listen . . . "

"Blue's hungry. I've got to feed him," he said abruptly. He marched into the kitchen and opened a can of Mongrel Meal, emptied it into Blue's bowl — it was his now — and set it down in front of his new buddy. Then he sat down to watch him eat, his mind racing furiously, going over again the things that bothered him about the dog and about the pictures that came snapping into his head without reason or warning.

Did the pictures come from Blue? Crazy idea. But say that the dog *was* able to send pictures, could it receive them also? This idea was even more crazy than the last. A telepathic dog! Who ever heard of a telepathic dog?

If Blue was telepathic, then it should be an easy matter to test him, Andy reasoned. He would think a command at the dog and if Blue obeyed the command, then it proved he was telepathic, didn't it? He wasn't sure. Maybe it wasn't the dog at all. Maybe it was Andy himself who was the weird one. Maybe all this pure country air was having a strange effect on him.

What command could he give? Something simple. He thought the words "lie down."

Blue continued to eat his Mongrel Meal. He was a noisy eater. Sounded like one of the hogs almost.

He thought harder. He pictured the two words in huge capital letters, black on a white background: LIE DOWN.

Nothing. Blue slurped his food.

Well that was that. The dog was not telepathic. Why did he feel so disappointed? It was a stupid idea anyway.

"Lie down!" said Andy in a loud voice.

"What?" called his mother from the other room.

"Talking to Blue," Andy yelled back.

The dog had almost emptied the bowl. What would happen, Andy wondered, if instead of words, he thought a picture of Blue lying down? Come to think of it, wasn't it kind of stupid of him to expect the dog to be able to read? But he might understand pictures. After all — he grew excited — it was pictures, not words, that he had been getting in his head!

He closed his eyes and concentrated. He thought of a picture of Blue lying down beside the bowl. He "sent" the picture to the dog.

The dog lay down.

Andy's heart thumped with excitement. He pictured Blue rolling over.

He sent the picture.

Blue rolled over.

Several times.

Then he bounded up at Andy enthusiastically,

forgetting about the food in his bowl. He gave a short bark of excitement, as if inviting Andy to play some more.

Andy gave a whoop of joy and threw his arms around the blue ball of wool and wrestled him to the floor and rolled and rolled and laughed with astonishment and happiness.

CHAPTER 8

After the boy and the dog had wrapped themselves around one another and after they had wrestled and rolled around the kitchen floor until they were completely hot and rolled-out, the boy leaped up and yelled, "Holy pig!"

"Andy?" His mother poked her head into the kitchen to see what all the noise was about.

He calmed himself, made his voice sound matter-of-fact. He needed more time to think. "I was playing with Blue." Which was true; he couldn't lie to his mother. He told her about his adventure with the sow instead, and when he had finished he said, "I should have noticed she was about to have babies, but I blew it."

"Was Mr. McAtee mad at you?"

Andy considered for a moment. He should admit to his mother that McAtee had been unexpectedly relaxed over the whole business, but instead, some demon inside him made him say, "He looked like his usual mean self, if that's what you mean."

"Everyone makes mistakes."

"He bawled out Uncle Ted."

"He must have deserved it."

"He was drinking."

His mother frowned.

"Said if he finds him drinking again he's finished."

"I was afraid something like this might happen. I'd better give your uncle a talking-to."

"He's sleeping in the barn. Maggoty wouldn't let him drive home."

"I'll go take a look at him and make sure he's all right."

This suited Andy. He wanted nothing more than to be left alone with Blue.

Alone with Blue again, he began to wonder if

he'd imagined everything so far. The dog looked so ordinary, so normal. Had the dog's behaviour been mere coincidence? He looked hard at Blue and pictured him getting up, walking over to him, and licking his left hand, which was lying on his knee. Just one lick. Blue stirred. Andy ran the picture through his mind again and sent it to Blue. The heap of blue curls lurched up from its spot on the rug, ambled over to Andy, and gave his right hand two licks instead of one. On the wrong hand. So the system wasn't perfect. But it would do. Of course it would do! He was the owner of a telepathic dog! Andy's stomach churned with excitement once again.

Later, as they all sat down to supper, his mother switched on the TV to see if their alien encounter would be at the top of the news. McAtee said he didn't think it would even get a mention. "News is only for entertainment, not for news," he said. "Besides, it's government 'top secret,' remember?"

He was right. No mention was made of the alien or his flying golfball.

Andy couldn't remember eating his supper. His mother and McAtee talked to him, but gave up when they had to keep repeating things. He couldn't wait for the meal to be over so he could be alone with Blue again.

His mother said to McAtee, "Andy didn't make the team."

McAtee said, "Hmmph."

She got up for more potatoes off the top of the stove, McAtee's eyes following her. Andy forgot about Blue for a moment and tried to see his mother as McAtee might be seeing her. She was slim, graceful, dark. Was she pretty? Possibly, though how could you look at your own mother the way others did, especially Maggoty? Maggoty liked her though, anyone could see that. He never said anything; he was always polite — Mrs. Scott this, Mrs. Scott that. But Andy saw the secret look burning in his eyes, and he didn't like it.

When the meal was finally over, Andy said, "Can Blue sleep in my room tonight?"

"The house is no place for a dog," said McAtee. "He'll be plenty warm in the shed with the collie."

"Blue is not a working dog like Finder, " said Andy, "he's a pet and he belongs to me and I want him to stay in the house."

"Andrew!" said his mother. "Mind your manners!"

"Mom, Patch slept in the kitchen and I see no

harm in Blue sleeping here too. Except tonight I've got things to talk over with him in my room. And I'm sorry for my manners, Mr. McAtee," he continued, turning to their employer, "but Blue is my friend — he's not just another useful worker and another mouth to feed."

"Andrew!" His mother was furious.

Before she could say any more McAtee got up from the table and reached into the refrigerator for a second bottle of beer. "You're right," he said, "I got no call to interfere. If you want the dog for a pet, that's fine by me, boy." He scowled. "Besides, seems to me the dog already earned his keep for the week when he scared that old sow into the farrowing crate."

Andy's mother flashed a quick look of thankful appreciation at McAtee.

McAtee flushed. "Dog's useful," he muttered hurriedly to hide his embarrassment.

Later, in his room, Andy sprawled on the top of his bed and gave Blue his full attention. What he needed to find out now was: did Blue *send* pictures as well as receive them? He already believed the answer to this question was yes, but he needed conclusive proof.

He had been figuring it all out during supper;

now he was ready to begin.

First he spoke quietly to Blue to get his attention. Then he pictured Patch, the friend he'd grown up with, the dog he had loved all his life. Next he pictured Patch padding along beside him, the way they'd gone everywhere together ever since Andy was just a little kid. Finally he pictured Patch in his arms, his coat matted with blood, head hanging limp, his body heavier in death than it had ever been in life.

He sent the pictures to Blue who sat watching his face.

He waited. He didn't know exactly what it was he was waiting for. A response. A communication. A sign that Blue had received and understood his message. He closed his eyes.

When the response came it shook him the way last night's storm had shaken the birches — down to the very roots.

The picture that snapped into his mind was sharp and clear. Tall blue grass rippled in the wind in a crazy landscape of black trees with strange, beckoning shapes. Dark purple sky the colour of ripe plums. Two moons. A man was walking over near the trees. The man was the alien, the one in the flying golfball — somehow he knew this — but the alien's eyes were not dulled in death the way he remembered them: they now glowed in the dark landscape almost the way a cat's eyes glow in the night.

The picture snapped off.

Immediately, another picture snapped in. It was one Andy had seen before, the alien lying dead in his transparent aircraft and Blue jumping up at him, and McAtee's big hand sweeping him aside like a whisk broom.

That was it. No more pictures. Andy had lost Patch. Blue had lost his master.

Andy wrapped his arms around Blue. "You're a lost dog all right," he mumbled, "and you're a long way from home. But now you live with me. You're mine. I'll take care of you from now on."

"Wuff," said Blue.

He had wanted a sign. He'd sure got it. The full impact of it all made him dizzy. Blue was from that alien planet with the two moons. Why hadn't anyone guessed that the dog and the alien were a pair? Why hadn't *he* guessed? He was the one who had the dream, who saw the picture in his mind of the alien's face before McAtee removed the helmet. He should have put two and two together. He could kick himself for his stupidity.

But Blue didn't really look like something from another planet. He looked like an earth dog. Except for his funny colour. The most amazing thing was that they had just finished swapping stories with one another. He had "told" Blue about Patch's death and Blue had come right back at him with his master's death. Incredible! They had communicated. Andy had a dog who dealt in pictures, telepathic pictures of startling, mind-shaking clarity!

"You sure fooled us all, Blue. Nobody figured it. A dog from outer space! What's the name of your planet? Where is it? How far away? Wait, let me think in pictures."

He concentrated. He pictured a planet in space. Then he pictured the flying golfball rocketing out of the planet.

He waited.

Nothing.

He pictured planet Earth as it is generally seen from outer space. Next he pictured a zoom from outer space, down, down, to the surface of the earth, and down to Andy Scott on the farm, sitting on his tractor.

Blue looked at him and wagged his tail as if to say, "I liked that." But no picture came back.

He concentrated again, this time making his mind a blank. He waited for a picture.

It came.

It was a picture of a moth fluttering around a bedside lamp. It was the sharpest picture so far, full of colour and fine detail.

He opened his eyes and the picture snapped off. It was his own bedside lamp. Blue was staring at a moth fluttering around the lamp.

Then Andy realized it had been different from the other pictures so far: it was as if he had been in Blue's mind looking at the world through Blue's eyes! He tried to get back in again, but couldn't. He concentrated, making his mind blank as he'd done before.

And he was in.

Snap! Like one of those press stud fasteners his mother had sewn on his pajamas (because he was always losing the buttons) he was looking through Blue's eyes at the moth again. The dog's full attention was caught by the moth's fluttering fascination with the light. Boy and dog were joined together as one mind.

Andy was one with Blue.

Gradually he was aware of other things: the tattoo of the moth's wings against the lampshade was louder and clearer to his ears. But the most amazing thing of all was the smell that flowed like a river through the open bedroom window — not only one smell, but a world of smells combined together, strong, scented, pungent, and wonderful!

And then he fell out of Blue's mind. The whole experience had been like climbing in one of Kirriemuir's old fruit trees, letting go of the branch, and dropping back to the ground.

Blue had stopped watching the moth, and was now lying sprawled on the window seat with his eyes closed.

Andy's heart and mind, like the wings of the moth, fluttered with excitement. But he had to stay calm. What had happened? He had made his mind a blank so that Blue could send him a picture. But Blue didn't happen to be sending a picture, the dog's mind was blank also. So Andy had been able to snap into Blue's mind, and had stayed for a few seconds — how many? — ten? twenty? — then he had fallen out again. It was magic. It was scary!

It was so scary he didn't want to repeat it. Not yet, anyhow. What if he did it again and got stuck in there and couldn't fall out? He shivered with fear and excitement. Not only could they send pictures to one another, but he could move into Blue's mind and see and smell and hear the world through the senses of a dog. The next question was: what was to be done about Blue? He was an alien animal. He was from outer space. He was telepathic. He had come in a flying golfball that had split apart and spilled him out into McAtee's yard. Wasn't Andy's duty to his government? Shouldn't he tell his mother and then have her call that Mr. Frost, the thin man who asked all the questions? He tried to think his way through his excitement and fear.

The answer was — nothing. He would do nothing. It would stay a secret between himself and Blue, at least for now. He couldn't tell anyone, not even his mother. It had to remain a secret, for he couldn't risk losing Blue to those sharp-faced special agents. They would take him away and cage him up like a specimen in a laboratory, an exhibit in a zoo. They'd prod him and poke him and shine lights into his eyes and take samples of his blood. And they would never let him go. The dog from outer space would be a prisoner, far away from home, condemned to a life sentence of loneliness without friends.

"Don't worry, Blue," he called to the dog in the window seat, "I won't let them take you away."

Blue jumped back onto the bed. Andy threw his arms around him. "I won't let them take you away," he said again. "I'll take care of you, you're mine now, I'll take care of you."

CHAPTER 9

He awoke later that night to the muffled thud of
McAtee's axe. Moonlight shone through the
window. Blue sat on the window seat looking
down at the yard. Andy groaned and sat up in bed.
He rubbed his eyes. The clock glowed 2:00. Blue
leaped onto the bed, wagging his tail.

"That mad Maggoty," Andy mumbled sleepily.
He slid out of bed and kneeled on the window seat,
his face up close to the glass. It was Maggoty all
right, stripped to the waist as before, his axe blade
flashing in the moonlight as he split one log after

another with powerful blows.

He was about to go back to bed when something white fluttered at the edge of his vision. He turned his head quickly toward the bay window below. It was his mother's room. He saw a ghostly figure, faceless in the dark, its white gown lit by the moonlight, and for a moment he thought it must be a ghost. But then he shook off the magical effect of the moon, and knew it was his mother. Standing back from her window (so she couldn't be seen by McAtee?), she was watching the strange nocturnal ritual of man and axe.

He stayed at the window, watching, for several minutes, until cold draughts drove him back to bed. He gave Blue a good-night scratch behind the ears. "Grownups are crazy," he said. Blue seemed to agree with him, for he sent Andy a picture of McAtee swinging his axe. Andy pulled the covers up over his chin and was soon asleep, dreaming of black beckoning trees, faceless ghosts floating over blue meadows, and giant warriors wielding flashing axeblades as they marched off to battle under double moons. "Kirriemuir! Kirriemuir!" they called with hollow voices.

The next day was Saturday. As soon as Andy opened his eyes he looked for Blue. The early morning sunshine filtered into the room through the yellow curtains of the small dormer window. He threw back the covers and almost fell out of bed in his eagerness to see and touch his new friend. Blue thrashed his tail.

"Picture time," said Andy, lying on the rug beside Blue. Because he wanted to learn more about that faraway home in the stars, he pictured Blue's world with its double moons and double shadows. Then he waited for Blue to pick it up.

But Blue made no response. Instead he ran back and forth around the room excitedly.

Should he try getting into Blue's head the way he'd been last night? That was scary. He was reluctant to try, especially with Blue acting so hyper this morning.

Blue ran to the open bedroom door, then came back to sit watching Andy. Then he sent a picture. It was a picture of the farmyard full of long morning shadows and the hayfield with breezes riffling through it like an ocean tide.

Andy laughed. "You want to get out into the sunshine."

He dressed quickly.

His mother was already downstairs in the kitchen nursing a cup of coffee, and McAtee was out working. Andy thought briefly about last night — his mother watching McAtee from her bedroom window — but now, in the light of day, it seemed unreal. Perhaps he'd dreamed it all. He filled Blue's bowl with water and set it down on the back steps. "Wait for me, Blue."

"Breakfast in five," said his mother. "Two over easy on rye and a side of hash browns." She liked to pretend she was back at the Lemon Tree sometimes. She seemed very unghostlike this morning in her blue plaid shirt and jeans.

"Nothing for me, Mom. I'll just get some milk. Blue wants to go for a run. You can give me a strip of bacon for him if you like."

"Now don't go spoiling that woolly blue mammoth, Andy. Feed a dog once a day, you know that."

When he got outside again, Andy said, "Mom says I mustn't spoil you, Blue." He knelt and threw his arms around the dog and hugged him to his chest. Assuming that he was being invited to a friendly wrestling match, Blue pushed and wriggled vigorously. Andy fell backwards with the dog on top of him. They rolled on the ground, locked together in happy confusion until Blue finally wriggled free and bounded away, then stopped, waiting for Andy to catch up.

The farm was freshly awake, its features blurred and soft with morning mists. The air was cool. The boy and his dog went together up and down and all around.

First they fed and watered the hogs. Then they visited the grumpy old sow and her baby pigs. When the sow saw Blue she gave a grunt of dislike and turned her head away.

The hay in the east field was ready for its second harvest, but would have to wait a few days until McAtee and Uncle Ted had finished the corn. All summer the hayfield had been a good place for Andy to hide, to relax and meditate; to consider the changing shapes of high white cumulus; and to listen to the drone of insects in the long grass.

It was also a good place for a boy and a dog to run. For they needed to get the proper measure of one another; and, as Andy had already learned, this could be discovered best by running. Running tested everything — the reflexes, the strength, the speed, the wind, and the heart. Especially the heart.

After a while, when they had run and shouted and barked enough, Andy called for time out.

They collapsed in the grass and sent pictures of good feeling to one another.

When they had recovered, Andy continued to lie stretched out in the tall grass with his hands behind his head and the sun on his eyelids. Blue's attention was caught, first by a Cabbage White butterfly fluttering drunkenly over the grass, and then by a flock of starlings settling down to gossip fifty yards away.

Andy had been putting it off, but now he was ready. He made his mind a blank. Concentrated. Picked up Blue's picture of starlings marching about and pecking at the earth.

And then — snap! He was in Blue's mind, watching the birds and trying to cope with the onslaught of sounds and smells.

Nature was full of sounds: buzzes and drones and clicks and chirps and scrapings and chitterings of every kind. It was a carpenter's shop, a zoo, an orchestra.

And the smells! He would never have guessed that tall, ripe grass could have such a sweet, sharp smell like burning incense, or that the earth could smell so rich and loamy, like a roomful of mushrooms.

Suddenly, Blue charged at the starlings. Andy's

viewpoint, about half a metre off the ground, didn't allow him to see much over the tall grass. But the starlings gave off a slightly acid aroma which was easy to follow. The grasses rushed by in a blur. The birds grumbled and took to the air reluctantly. Blue stopped and barked at them and thrashed his tail.

Which was when Andy fell out. He looked around. He was alone. "Blue," he called. The dog came trotting back. Andy's heart was beating fast, whether from the scary strangeness of it all or from the excitement of the chase or what, he didn't know. Nor could he figure out this strange mind transfer business. Could Blue get into his mind as easily as he got into Blue's? And when he was in Blue's mind, who was in control, himself or the dog? Getting out felt, as before, like falling. Perhaps he would learn control with more practice.

He jumped up, full of excitement. They ran down to the river. It wasn't much of a river, more like a creek. Andy threw a stick upstream. "Fetch it, Blue!" Blue didn't move. Andy sent him a picture of Patch retrieving a stick from the river. Blue stood on the bank and barked with fright at the sluggish currents. Andy threw several sticks and several pictures, but nothing had any effect.

Blue sent a picture. A surging, inky river rushed madly over black rocks. It was Blue's world with its twin moons, only this time the moons were bigger and brighter and hung over the river like klieg lights on a movie set. Out of the foam leaped a huge silver fish with terrible jaws. It lashed its tail and plunged beneath the swirling waters. The picture faded.

Andy patted Blue's shoulder. "OK — no swimming. I get the picture." He could see that he and Blue had much to learn from each other.

After lunch he helped his mother in the vegetable patch. Blue wandered off to explore on his own. After he had been working for a while, Andy leaned his chin on the handle of his hoe and closed his eyes. Where was Blue? He blanked his mind and searched for him. The picture came: Blue was watching the chickens. Could he move into Blue's mind from this distance? He vaulted in, snap! It was getting easier even at a distance. Then — panic!

Blue was being threatened by a strutting rooster who didn't like strangers in his yard. Blue backed off. Andy felt the thrill of conflict as he looked right into the rooster's mean, yellow eye. Blue barked, warning him away. The rooster kept on coming, his comb and wattles a bright indignant red and his neck feathers bristling with anger. Blue stood his ground. The rooster drew nearer. Andy could smell its sharp sawdust odour, and—

— saw the picture that Blue threw at the rooster just a second before he fell out of the dog's head in fright. It was a ferocious, fox-like creature with mad red eyes and sword teeth, and it was reaching out with razor claws. He also saw in that second the screaming rooster half run, half fly from Blue in mortal terror.

Andy was back, leaning on the hoe. He wiped the sweat from his brow with the back of his hand. His mother was there looking at him anxiously. "Are you all right?"

"Sure, Mom, why?"

"You've been leaning on that hoe so long with your eyes closed I thought maybe you were sick."

"Sorry. I let my mind wander off. "

He shook his head. Now he understood why the old sow had broken off her thundering charge in the pasture last night. He chuckled to himself. Starlings and roosters, moths and butterflies, silver alien fish, and now an alien fox-monster! Blue's home turf must be a really interesting place. He chuckled again. Letting his mind wander off was more fun than his mother would ever know!

CHAPTER 10

"Looks like another storm brewing, Lucy," Uncle Ted said to his sister-in-law as he took his place at the table.

Uncle Ted was staying for dinner. Then he was going to work overtime with McAtee to get the big cornfield harvested. They planned to work to ten or eleven o'clock. "This time of year," he explained to Andy, "if there's too much moisture left in the corn it won't store well for the winter. And with the chance of another storm, we've got to bring it in or . . ." He left the words hanging.

Andy said, "Can I help?"

Uncle Ted turned to McAtee with raised eyebrows. McAtee said nothing. "Don't see as why not," said Uncle Ted. "You could drive the small tractor-trailer. That be OK, Lucy?"

Andy looked at his mother. He thought she looked pretty this evening in her white shirtwaist dress, her dark hair tied back with a blue ribbon. Kirriemuir had been good to her, he realized. Gone was that thin, dusty look of the city. Now she glowed with colour and good health. She was sitting across the table from McAtee. Andy sat on her left and Uncle Ted was to her right. Every so often she had to get up for something for the table and whenever she did, McAtee's eyes followed her. His eyes looked darker than ever and they glowed with a strange smouldering fire.

Andy watched him from the corner of his eye. He felt a hot, angry fear rise up inside of him and he wanted to smash McAtee's face with his fists, wanted to tell him to keep his eyes off his mother. He could tell by the smallest stiffness in his mother's back and by the set of her head that she was fully conscious of McAtee's stare. And when she sat down, pulling in her chair and smoothing her dress, her own eyes met McAtee's and seemed to glow with that same soft fire. Silence hung over the table like a summer heat, pressing down on all of them. Then she spoke. "It's up to Mr. McAtee," she said.

McAtee tore his eyes from hers and growled, "It won't be necessary for the boy to help. Too many accidents at night with machinery."

Andy looked across at his uncle, but Uncle Ted avoided his eyes, pretending instead a sudden interest in the blade of his table knife. Andy pleaded silently with his mother for support, but she frowned at him.

He was on his own. He stared boldly at McAtee. "I'm careful," he said in a level voice.

McAtee spoke quietly. "I said no."

Andy felt a stab of hatred for this man who ruled all their lives, this cruel master whose every word was law at Kirriemuir. His food stuck in his throat; he wanted to spit it out. He stood up from the table, dizzy, the blood suddenly pounding in his temples. He couldn't trust himself to speak. McAtee the tormentor. His mother and his uncle cowed and silent. He twisted blindly away from the table, sending his chair crashing to the floor, and threw himself out of the house.

Blue followed.

Outside, the sky was dark with the gathering storm; thick clouds roiled overhead. Blue trotted at his heels as they crossed the barnyard. He didn't know where he was going. All he knew was that he had to get away from the terrible sight of McAtee and his mother with their eyes locked together, away from McAtee's domineering cruelty. To him he was only "boy." He marched quickly, his teeth and fists clenched.

Suddenly in front of them appeared the big strutting rooster, barring their way, its neck feathers bristling. This was the same king of the barnyard who had earlier flown from Blue's monster picture. Now he reminded Andy of McAtee, the king of Kirriemuir.

"Go get him, Blue!" growled Andy.

The rooster's comb and wattles turned a bright red as it advanced on dog and boy.

"Kill!" yelled Andy. "Kill!"

His mind snapped into the dog's mind.

And he was glaring at the rooster's yellow eyes and could smell its acid-sawdust anger. "Kill!" he thought. "Kill!"

Blue launched himself at the angry rooster. Andy felt the rooster's sharp talons rake and tear his shoulder muscles as he clamped his sharp teeth around the rooster's skinny neck. Blue gave a shake of his head and broke the rooster's neck with a snap. Andy tasted the blood in his jaws, sweet and hot, felt the thrill of victory in his mouth and heart.

He let the dead rooster drop.

The limp carcass fell in the barnyard dust and twitched several times. The yellow eyes stared sightlessly at the thickening clouds.

Andy fell out of Blue's mind and out of the sweet and sickly smell of death.

Blue barked with excitement and pain. "Take it easy," Andy croaked. He reached down, touching the dog to calm him. But he couldn't calm the pounding in his own throat, or the trembling in his limbs. Killing an angry rooster with your teeth was not the same as crushing cockroaches with your shoe. His fingers came away from the dog's shoulder sticky with blood, Blue's blood. He stared. He couldn't see clearly in the lowering darkness, but he remembered the rooster's claws and the pain. Now his whole body was trembling. He stumbled back toward the house.

He pushed his way into the kitchen. Blue followed. He could hear his mother talking to Uncle Ted in the living room. McAtee had gone out. He soaked a towel and knelt beside Blue. He tried to clean off the blood, but the wounded dog shied away and instead curled up in a corner and licked at the wound with his long tongue. "Sorry, Blue," he whispered. "I'll never do anything like that again, I promise." He tried sending a picture, but nothing happened. Blue licked at his wound.

Uncle Ted clumped into the kitchen. "Andy? I been looking all over for you. Mr. McAtee says maybe if you haven't changed your mind about helping tonight you could haul corn with us."

Andy looked over at Blue. The dog lay drawn up into himself, his head turned away from them, still and silent.

Uncle Ted pulled at his nose. "But you'll have to be careful out there. Mr. McAtee was worried, sure enough. Accidents happen real easy when its dark and a feller gets all wore out. But that small trailer would cut an hour off our haulin' time. You game?"

"Sure," said Andy, "I'll help."

"Be careful out there," said his mother, who had followed Uncle Ted into the kitchen.

"I'll be careful," said Andy.

CHAPTER 11

The cornfield at night was an unfamiliar jungle of towering stalks. Lit by the spotlights on the harvester and the two tractors, the thick, leafy forest had a fantastical quality about it more frightening than its daylight guise.

Blue had not followed Andy out to work. Blue didn't kill other animals. Blue didn't need to, for he frightened them off with harmless pictures. Andy was the killer. He was no better than McAtee who had killed Patch.

He sat slumped on his tractor, watching Uncle

Ted's tractor and wagon leave the field with a load of corn for the silo. When McAtee gave the signal by waving his arm, Andy took Uncle Ted's place, pulling the empty wagon so it sat underneath the spout of the combine. The shelled corn poured into the wagon, four tonnes of it, the colour of gold under the harvester lights. When the wagon was full, he headed for the silo. By this time, Uncle Ted was back for another load. He gave Andy a salute as he roared by.

The wind was starting to get up. The cornstalk jungle began to shift and toss about like kelp on a coral reef.

Three hours later the wind was gale force. Andy was finished. All the corn was in. Gusting winds made it difficult to stand upright. He started to help his uncle unload his corn at the silo. Uncle Ted staggered and fell against his tractor.

"Here, let me," said Andy, bracing himself against the wind. He switched on the blower that would send the corn thirty metres up the feeder tube into the top of the silo, and began to unload his uncle's wagon.

His uncle was singing something. The words were lost in the wind.

When the corn was unloaded, Andy shut off the

blower motor. His uncle was sitting on the ground, his back against a tractor wheel, drinking from a bottle of whiskey. The bottle was almost empty. He took the bottle from his lips and held it out to Andy. He was drunk.

Andy snatched the bottle and hurled it away into the windy night. "You've got to put your tractor away, Uncle Ted, before Maggoty sees you!"

"I dream of Jeannie," sang Uncle Ted.

Andy helped him to his feet and pushed him up onto the tractor. His uncle resisted.

"Gotta cap the silo, Andy," he slurred. "Can't go leave cap offa th'silo." He struggled back down.

"Leave it to me," said Andy, "and get back before Maggoty finds you. You're drunk. He'll fire you for sure. Get back!" He pushed him onto the tractor seat, tears of desperation in his eyes.

"Gotta cap th' corn," mumbled Uncle Ted.

"How do I do it? Tell me!"

His uncle leaned down, his eyes glazed. He pointed to the top of the silo. "Up the monkey ladder, m'boy. Bolt the cap shut nice and tight so the corn don't get wet." He started the tractor. ". . . Jeannie . . . light brown hair," he sang over the roar of the tractor and the wind, " . . . borne like a vapour on the summer air." He drove off toward the tractor shed.

Andy's heart sank into his leather workboots. He would have to climb that long ladder upward in the darkness and howling wind and bolt shut the cap that kept air and rain out of the silo. Or else he could get McAtee to do it, which meant Uncle Ted would be fired. He considered. He could leave it until tomorrow, for the daylight. The small amount of rain that would get into the blower hole could do no real harm to the corn, could it? He wasn't sure. Didn't his uncle say something about too much moisture in the corn? What if the rain poured in and ruined the whole crop! He had no choice. He had to go up. Damn Uncle Ted! And damn McAtee! The sensible thing would be to go back to the field and tell McAtee he couldn't climb because of his fear of heights, and that Uncle Ted was sick. But McAtee wouldn't be fooled by this story. He'd fire Uncle Ted and call Andy a coward.

Which he was.

He was a coward.

Heights had always made him sick, as far back as he could remember. He got dizzy and broke out in a sweat and his legs gave way and he always knew he was going to fall down, down, down.

Andy slumped in the tractor seat, remembering.When he and Morgie were in the fourth grade, they had gone swimming at the St. John Simmons public pool on Angel Street with a bunch of other kids, one afternoon after school. Everyone had climbed the long ladder up to the high diving board, jumping off one at a time into the pool a million kilometres below. Andy climbed onto the platform and looked down.

A terrible weakness swept over him. He almost fell. If it hadn't been for Morgie, he would have died then and there. Morgie was just behind him, for when Andy had walked out onto the platform, Morgie had waited on the top of the ladder for him to make his leap.

He thought he was going to be sick. He staggered, clutched at the rail, and collapsed onto the coconut matting. Morgie yelled down at the other kids strung out behind to get off the ladder, then he helped him back down, slowly, painfully, until they were safely back on the ground. The other kids started to laugh and jeer, but Morgie fixed them with one of his looks and they shut up. But things were never the same at school after that. He always felt that the kids talked behind his back and called him a coward.

That word. Coward.

Now, looking up at the silo ladder, much higher than the one at the St. John Simmons swimming pool, he wondered if he could do it. Nobody was watching to see him fail. Nobody was there to call him coward.

He had to do it. For Uncle Ted.

The silo ladder started three metres from the ground. To reach the ladder he drove his tractor under the bottom rungs and turned his engine off. He switched of all but one of the lights. Then he reached up to the guardrail and pulled himself onto the bottom step of the ladder.

He took two steps up the ladder and stopped. The night was black and thick like crankcase oil. His stomach knotted with tension. The wind howled high up at the top of the silo. He looked down. The tractor light was aimed at the base of the silo. Already the ground looked far away. He began his climb. He rose slowly, step by step, his hands cold on the metal handrail. He didn't look down but kept climbing into the wind and the darkness.

After a while, he stopped and hooked his elbows through the rails to relieve his cold hands. He opened and closed his fists and blew on his hands to warm them. He glanced down. The tractor light was now only a faint glow in the darkness below. He shivered, and felt that old familiar weakness creeping over him. He wanted to clamber back down to the light and safety. He looked up at the ladder stretching away into the darkness, then clenched his jaw, gripped the handrail, and continued his climb.

The edge of the wind clutched at him from around the side of the silo. He felt the first rain on his face. He inched up slowly, one step at a time, until he finally reached the top. There the full force of the wind shrieked through the guardrail and leaped at his chest like a wild boar.

He pulled himself up and over the top with the wind tearing at him, threatening to sweep him off the tower and send him whirling away like a leaf. Now he was standing on his feet. He grasped the rail tighter with icy fingers and pushed himself forward to the blower hole at the silo's centre. On the other side of the guardrail the silo roof sloped sharply down so that, as he stood shivering at the edge of the hole with his hands gripping the rail, he could only dimly discern the metal roof falling away into the night. He was trapped. On the other side of the rail was a thirty-metre drop to the ground. On this side of the rail there was the gaping blower hole, like a dark mouth waiting to swallow him down into the stomach of the huge silo.

He trembled with fear and fatigue and cold.

He tried to move toward the steel cap which lay on the roof, attached to the rail by a short length of safety cable, but his legs collapsed. It was just like that time on the high diving board. He hooked one arm through the rail and clasped the wrist with the other hand and held on tight. He was kneeling now, head down, eyes closed against the wind and the rain. He forced himself to drag air into his lungs. His heart was hammering.

He raised his head. The cap was only a metre away. He inched forward on his knees, still clinging to the wet rail. He reached for the cable with one hand and pulled the cap toward him. The cap was heavy. He pushed at it with his feet. When he had it in position near the hole, he reluctantly let go of the rail and stretched out on his stomach. The steel deck was cold and wet. His teeth were chattering. He pushed the cap into place and, with shaking fingers, tightened the bolt.

It was done.

He lay there for several minutes trying to still the wild thumping in his breast. The rain beat a tattoo on his back. He felt his way back to the rail again and tried to stand, but his legs refused to support him. Another wave of dizziness and nausea rolled over him. He wanted to die in the deep cold darkness under the stinging rain and the cutting wind. He'd never make it back down the ladder, for there was no feeling in his legs and his frozen arm was locked through the rail and he didn't seem to be able to release it.

Somewhere in the far distance, carried by the wind across the wide fields, came the faint barking of a dog. Blue. Or Finder. Couldn't tell which. Didn't matter which. Too far away. Never make it down. No strength. No feeling in hands and legs. Sick. Uncle Ted would be on his way home by now. Nobody would know he was on top of the silo. But when it got very late McAtee would search for him, wouldn't he? And he'd find the tractor at the foot of the silo and then he would know. Eventually. And he'd find his broken body beside it, toppled off the silo because he was too frozen and too weak to hold on. And too much of a coward to make it down on his own.

He hugged the rail and drew his knees up into

his stomach. If only he could hold on, McAtee would eventually find him. McAtee always cleaned everything up before putting things away for the night. He would come eventually. Maybe as he was sitting down, just about to enjoy a beer, Andy's mother would say, "Where's Andy?" And McAtee would look surprised and say, "He's not in bed?" But by then it would be too late.

Or maybe Blue would pluck his thought pictures of distress out of the stormy air. He tried making his mind a blank so he could vault into Blue's mind just as he did with the rooster, but nothing happened. He was exhausted. But he concentrated on a picture of himself and sent it out into the blackness. Blue would save him. If he wasn't too far away. How far could thoughts travel before they were swept away by the wind like sparrows with broken wings?

Again came the faint faraway bark of a dog. But he didn't hear it, for he was beyond hearing and beyond caring. With his head resting against his locked arm, eyes closed, he had given himself up to the fear and fatigue and the terrible cold.

CHAPTER 12

He was dimly aware that someone was yelling at him.

The familiar gruff voice was pitched three or four octaves below the shriek of the wind.

McAtee. Standing over him, bracing himself against the force of the wind. He wore a rope around his middle. At the end of the rope was a harness-snap clipped to the rail as insurance against slipping boots and gusting wind.

Andy lay curled up on the top of the rain-slicked deck of the silo with one arm hooked through the metal rail. McAtee crouched down and looped a second rope around the boy's chest, and secured it to his own waist. Then he swept him up and tossed him over his shoulder as easily as a sack of grain. The descent was slow. McAtee clipped and unclipped the harness-snap on the ladder rungs, taking only a few steps at a time. When McAtee finally reached the ground, Andy didn't see Blue jumping up at him, for by this time he had passed out. Nor was he aware of the ride to the house in the pickup. He remembered nothing until he came to in his own bed. It was the word *hypothermia* spoken by that same gruff voice that filtered into his consciousness.

"People die from low body temperature. How long was he up there?" His mother's voice. She was holding his hand on the bedcovers. Her hand was warm.

"I reckon over an hour. But he'll be OK." McAtee.

"Thanks be to God." His mother.

Silence. He kept his eyes closed, not ready to open them yet; he needed time to think.

"And thanks to you too, Mr. McAtee. I didn't thank you." His mother was weeping softly.

So it was McAtee who had brought him down.

He hadn't been imagining things. McAtee knew now what a coward he was. He felt the shame like a hot thing all over his skin. He should have died of hypo-whatever-it-was. He wanted to open his eyes, but he wasn't ready yet for McAtee's eyes telling him that awful truth.

"No thanks needed, Mrs. Scott."

"I don't know what made him do it. He's acrophobic. Andy's always had a fear of heights. Wouldn't ride on my shoulders when he was a baby without fussing and yelling and cutting up."

He almost cried out in surprise. Acrophobic? He didn't know he was that. Fear of heights yes, but he hadn't known that his mother knew all about it all along. Then why had they never discussed it?

McAtee was saying something. He sounded angry.

"Then what the heck was he trying to prove?"

"Perhaps he was trying to prove something to you, Mr. McAtee."

"To *me?*" McAtee's voice went up a whole octave. "Boy's got nothing to prove to me!" He started to make a noise that sounded to Andy suspiciously like a chuckle. "I could see he had grit the first day when he faced up to me over the working dog, the collie. And then later, the way he threw himself between that dog of his and my shotgun, even though I had no mind to shoot the thing." He chuckled again. "I've always known the boy's got grit."

Andy couldn't believe what he was hearing! First, it was the longest speech he'd ever heard McAtee make. Second, *the boy's got grit!* Grit was the same as guts wasn't it? The boy's got guts. He liked McAtee's word better. *Grit.*

So he wasn't a coward? Cowards didn't have grit. He felt a surge of happiness. He had to keep himself from smiling.

McAtee's voice had been mumbling on. He listened. " . . . the boy's father," said McAtee.

"Tim Scott was no good," he heard his mother say. "He couldn't keep a job. All Tim ever wanted was a bottle in his hand and a crowd around him — especially women! Everyone liked him, but he was weak. Walked out one night with another woman and never came back."

McAtee said, "Hmmph."

"I was better off without him."

"Does the boy know?"

"I never told him. Andy thinks his father died fighting in Ireland. A hero. Better that way than always have him blame me for his father walking out on him."

Andy listened in torture. He lay still, his eyes closed and his heart shrinking. His father not a war hero but a bum. She had to be lying. It wasn't true. Not his father. He lay with his eyes closed. His mind flooded with aching memories of his father. He was only a little kid when his father left, hadn't even started kindergarten. He remembered playing on the old Electrolux vacuum cleaner, sitting astride it like a horse and pushing it along on its runners, making engine noises, pretending it was a ship or an ambulance or a jumbo jet. "All clear on runway number two," his father would call out, "prepare to land." Or "Ambulance unit 437, pick up a black-and-white puppy, name of Patch, broken tail, bring him in for X-ray and vitamins, over."

His father died a hero in a war. He'd always believed that. But now he knew the truth. And the truth stabbed him like a knife through the heart.

His mother had kept that awful secret to herself all these years. He wanted to cry for himself and for his mother.

She let go of his hand.

Silence.

He risked a peep through one eye. They were looking at each other in that way again, pouring their eyes helplessly. McAtee was standing at the foot of the bed and she was staring up at him, her lips parted. McAtee came over to her, placed his hands on her shoulders and slowly raised her up. He stood looking at her for the longest time. Then he bent down and kissed her on the lips.

She kissed him back.

Andy closed his eyes tight shut and lay there listening to the silence. Then . . .

"Quinn, I'm . . . "

"I want you to stay here, Lucy. For always. This is your home now, you and the boy. You know that don't you?"

"Yes, I know."

"I love you, Lucy."

"I know. But Andy . . . "

Silence. He peeped.

They were kissing again.

He made a few grunting noises, pretending to awake. He felt his mother's hand on his again. "Where's Blue?" he groaned. He opened his eyes.

His mother's face was flushed with happiness. Because her son was recovering? Or because she was in love with Quinn McAtee?

At the sound of Andy's voice Blue hurled himself up onto the bed, licked his young master's face, and gave several excited yaps. And zapped Andy with a picture: dozens of strings of coloured lights danced in ascending spirals against a purple sky. The colours were mostly shimmering pinks and blues, and could have been fireflies or luminous birds. Whatever they were, they made Andy feel happy and warm. He began to forget the heaviness in his heart over his father and the confused feelings he had about his mother kissing McAtee. He threw his arms around Blue and hugged him and tenderly felt the rooster wound on his shoulder.

"How do you feel, Andy?" His mother's eyes were shining. Her hand felt hot.

"I'm fine, Mom."

"Your Uncle Ted had no business sending you up that awful tower on a night like this. He'll get a tongue-lashing tomorrow if he dares show his face in this house. It's a good thing he told Quinn — Mr. McAtee — "

"Ted told me nothing," said McAtee, "I didn't see him."

"Then how did you know Andy was on the silo?"

Andy looked into McAtee's eyes. McAtee looked

back at him. His face wore a puzzled frown. Mc-Atee said, "The small tractor wasn't in the shed so I knew the boy was out there somewhere, but I wasn't worried none. Andy's a capable young feller, so I figured he'd bring her in when he was good and ready." McAtee stopped and scratched his head. "Then the strangest thing — the dog . . . "

"Blue," said Andy.

The dog's ears pricked up at the sound of his name.

"Blue." McAtee nodded. "Came a-barking at me like it had something on its mind, and that was when I saw the boy lying on the top of the silo. Plain as this hand." He stared at his palm.

"Go on," said Andy's mother.

McAtee sat down on the end of the bed, still staring at his palm. "It was like a dream, except it wasn't a dream. I know now what it was. It was a message. . . . "

"From Blue," said Andy.

"From God," said his mother. She stared at McAtee. He stared at her.

"Blue," said Andy again.

They didn't hear him. The flush at his mother's throat made her look young, like a girl almost.

"Mom, it was Blue. He's an alien animal from

that flying golfball. And he's telepathic some-
times. He's not smarter than Patch or other dogs,
I don't think, but he's sure different. That's why
Mr. McAtee saw me up on the silo. I sent a picture
to Blue and Blue sent it to him. You get it? It was
Blue."

But he might as well have been talking in
Turkish. His mother and McAtee were just pouring their eyes again. Andy sighed.

His mother heard the sigh. "Can I get you some
hot . . ."

"I think I'll just go back to sleep. I'm tired." He
was finding it hard to keep his eyes open. Blue
sent him a picture of a pair of swallows swooping
and darting over the hayfield, chasing each other.
Andy laughed sleepily.

Only Blue saw McAtee take Lucy Scott's hand
and lead her out of the room. Andy was already
asleep.

CHAPTER 13

On Sunday he felt better. He insisted that he could manage his usual chores, but McAtee said no, that his uncle could take care of the hogs for a couple of days or so. Which meant that Andy had the day off. He loaded Blue into the passenger seat of his mother's old Pontiac, which mostly sat idle out in the yard, and they spent the afternoon bumping over mown fields and up and down the rutted driveways between them.

On Monday he went to school. Coach Taylor singled him out. "I want you for the track and field team, Scott, OK?" Before Andy had time to answer, Coach Taylor said, "Be on the track tomorrow, half-past three."

"Right, Coach," said Andy, but the coach had gone. Cliff Anderson, standing nearby, gave him the thumbs up sign. Andy felt good. When he got home, his mother and McAtee were drinking coffee in the kitchen, facing one another across the table.

"Your dog killed the rooster," growled McAtee as soon as he walked in. "You're going to have to let him go."

"Let him go?" Andy didn't understand.

McAtee looked down at his boots. "He'll have to be put down."

"Kill Blue?" He felt his heart sink.

"Dog's no good on a farm once he gets a taste for killing." McAtee was still looking down at his boots.

"How do you know it was Blue?"

"Rooster got its claws on him."

Andy straightened his shoulders. He no longer feared or hated this man. Maybe it was the storm, or maybe it was the killing of the rooster, but whatever it was, something had changed between them. "Mr. McAtee," he said, looking him straight in the eyes, "what if I told you it wasn't Blue that killed the rooster, that it was me?"

McAtee said nothing. He waited for Andy to finish.

"Because that's exactly what happened. I *made* Blue kill the old rooster. I was angry and I — " He paused. McAtee looked sideways at Andy's mother. Andy knew it was useless to try to explain what had really happened. They could never understand. " — I set him on the rooster. And I can promise you it will never happen again," he finished.

McAtee searched the boy's face. "I believe you," he said. "But if the dog kills again, he has got to go. OK?"

Andy felt a great weight lift from his chest. He smiled at McAtee. "OK," he said.

That night, he felt better about himself and his mother and Kirriemuir than he had felt since their move from the city. He fell quickly into a deep, peaceful sleep as soon as his head hit the pillow.

In the early hours of the morning, silver moonlight cast long shadows across the room and over the bed where he lay. Blue arose from his spot on the rug and padded over to the window. He jumped up onto the windowseat and sat looking out at the full moon. He sat there quietly for several minutes.

The hoot of a brown owl came hollowly up from beyond the birches and was followed by a fainter, answering hoot from the country graveyard.

Blue jumped down to the floor and trotted silently out the bedroom door and down the stairs. He nosed the latch off the back door and bounded out past the piles of workboots into the yard.

It wasn't the bright moonlight on Andy's face that woke him, it was the humming sound outside his window. He sat up and listened. The hum was steady and low, like the whirr of an electric motor. He slid out of bed and hurried over to the window. He gasped. The farmyard was bathed in moonlight. But it wasn't this that caused his mouth to gape open in astonishment. Hovering over the yard, about twenty metres up in the air, was a flying saucer.

It couldn't have been anything else.

About as wide as the farmhouse, it was the real thing this time, not a golfball. With its thin, circular shape, its domed centre, and its ring of pulsing blue light, it was the alien ship from outer space that everyone knows from movies and comic strips and news reports. And he was staring at it now as it hovered in his own back yard.

Underneath the ship, on the ground, sat Blue watching the ship's slow descent.

Andy fought his way into his trousers, grabbed his sweatshirt and pulled it on over his head as he flew down the stairs. He thumped his fist on McAtee's door. "Flying saucer!" he yelled.

His mother's bedroom was next to McAtee's. She flung her door open. "Andy! What is it?"

"Flying saucer!" He was choking with excitement. He turned and ran.

"Andrew! Come back!"

But he kept going. He flung himself out the back door and pushed his bare feet into his cold workboots. His mother and McAtee were right behind him. When they saw the spaceship they stared. "It *is* a flying saucer!" his mother gasped.

"Blue!" yelled Andy. "Come back here!" But the dog's attention didn't waver from the descending spacecraft. Andy concentrated: he pictured Blue obeying his command. Nothing happened. No return transmission, and no way to know if Blue was picking up his order. He started forward to retrieve the dog.

"No, wait," said McAtee clamping his big hand

around Andy's shoulder. "You can't go out there."

"Blue could get hurt, burned maybe," Andy cried.

"Leave him be," said McAtee.

"Quinn, shouldn't we call the police?"

"Not yet, Lucy. If this contraption is from the same place as the other one then maybe they're just searching for it." He gave a bear-like growl. "Besides, if you call the police we'll have those other fools swarming all over the place again."

"But we must do something," said Andy's mother. "Quinn, I'm scared."

McAtee said nothing. He put his arm around her shoulders and stood watching the spaceship calmly.

"They've come for Blue," said Andy. He felt like crying.

"Blue?" McAtee growled. "Why would they be coming for the dog?"

"I told you already. He's an alien dog. He came in the golfball. They've come back for him."

His mother and McAtee stared at the dog sitting out in the yard. Then they looked at one another. Then they stared at Andy.

His mother's voice shook. "Andy, are you saying that you weren't making all that up? About Blue?"

"He's from outer space." Andy nodded.

The humming sound ceased as the saucer alighted gently on the ground. They waited quietly. Andy's mother looped her arm around her son's shoulder. They watched and waited.

The pulsing blue light around the rim of the saucer dimmed to a purple glow. Blue sat quietly watching.

"Let me go get him," Andy pleaded. "It's not dangerous now."

"Wait," whispered his mother.

They waited.

The moon daubed everything with its silver brush: the people and the dog, and the huge, pulsing spacecraft that had come from some strange and distant star to Kirriemuir Farm.

CHAPTER 14

They waited, not taking their eyes off the ship from outer space.

A door in the side of the dome slid open. The light inside the ship was blue. An alien stepped out and stood facing them. Andy couldn't see him clearly, but the silhouette was that of a small, thin person. He wore no helmet. His face was in darkness.

Blue barked. The alien turned and looked down at the dog and as he did so the moonlight fell on his face. He had enormous, owl-like eyes. He was just like the other one, Blue's master, who had died in the shattered golfball.

Andy guessed that the alien and Blue were communicating with each other. Blue looked over towards Andy as if trying to decide something.

"Here, Blue!" Andy called.

And Blue came.

He bounded away from the spaceship and into Andy's waiting arms. "Good boy, Blue," he whispered in the dog's ear.

Andy's mother held on to McAtee more tightly. The alien stood facing them from the deck of his ship, his face in darkness once again.

The words crept into Andy's mind like gentle fingers massaging his scalp. Except that they weren't really words, more like musical pictures in some rich, new language. He understood the language without any difficulty. The strange musical words were honouring him, and they promised to take him one day to their alien world.

"You would wish this?"

"A visit? Yes."

"Then one day when you are full-grown we will come for you."

"Why are you here?"

"You know why we are here."

"Blue wants to stay here with me."

"We are sorry. The animal is not of this world."

"I need him. Let him stay."

"We are sorry. It is the law. We can leave nothing on an outworld. Once, many years ago, we left a *ruum*. It was an accident. The *ruum* caused much trouble with your animal life. We can leave nothing here. That is the law."

"What about the dead one who crashed? He has been left here. His body was taken to the hospital. And the golfball, what about that?"

"The golfball as you call it has been . . . vapourized. It is no longer here in your world. As for its pilot, she too is as the air."

"She?"

"Yes. Her name was Lela."

"You have taken her body, and now you want to take Blue away from me."

"It must be."

"Andy, you're trembling," said his mother. "What is it?"

"The alien is using telepathy," said Andy. "Don't you hear him?"

"I hear nothing," said McAtee.

"Mother?"

She shook her head.

"The aliens are taking Blue back with them," he explained.

"Tell them the dog lives here," growled McAtee.

"It's no good," said Andy, "there's nothing we can do." He unwrapped his arms from around the dog. "You've got to go home, Blue."

A picture clicked into his head. It was from Blue. He saw a city of tall blue glass towers. It was evening. Twin moons, one violet, the other a misty lavender, hung over the city. Blue was remembering his home planet. Or perhaps it was Blue's way of asking Andy to come with him to his world.

"It's no good, Blue, I can't come with you." He formed a picture of himself under the Earth moon and sent it to Blue.

The dog whimpered.

"Goodbye, Blue." He ran his fingers through the dog's soft coat for the last time. "I'm gonna miss you."

The tingling word-music came again.

"We will return here one day. I am called Karam. I too am woman. Please stand away from the animal."

Andy stood and backed off as Blue was enveloped in a luminous purple light. Then the light, with Blue inside it, began to move slowly away from Andy toward the spacecraft. He could see Blue biting and snapping at the bubble. When the dog saw he couldn't escape he sat quietly looking out at Andy, his eyes full of sorrow and loss.

The bubble increased its speed, gliding in a slow arc to the spaceship door. Just before it disappeared into its interior, Andy received Blue's last picture. It was the swallows again, darting and swooping over the hayfield, chasing one another out of sight so that, except for the breeze riffling the silky stems of the tall grass, the hayfield was empty.

The hayfield was empty.

The alien raised an arm in salute, then turned and disappeared into the ship. The door slid closed. The blue lights around the ship's perimeter glowed and pulsed with the increasing hum of the ship's engines. The spacecraft rose, slowly at first, up over the farmhouse roof, then faster until it suddenly rocketed away and disappeared into the night.

Andy could see the lights for a few seconds only. Then nothing. Blue was gone. Back to his home in the stars. The face of the silver moon seemed to be mocking him and the rest of the sky was vast and empty and silent. Blue was gone into the faceless ocean of dust and stars. They would never see one another again.

His mother gave his shoulders a squeeze.

McAtee said, "Don't take it too hard, son. Dogs are happier on the piece of land they were raised on. They'll take care of him."

They walked back to the house.

CHAPTER 15

Work at Kirriemuir slowed after the harvest. But there were still some year-end plums and pears and apples to pick from the few gnarled old trees, and tomatoes heavy and plump on the vine, and the air was full of a pleasant, dusty, overripe heaviness.

The evenings, however, were cold. The work with the animals was never finished, for that went on all the year round. McAtee took care of the cattle and Andy the hogs. Andy made no further mistakes with the farrowing sows, for he was developing an expert eye for the animals in his care.

Uncle Ted helped wherever he was needed. He had done no further drinking since the night of the silo. Andy never did tell on him, though he threatened to tell all if his uncle brought liquor to work with him ever again. Andy's mother gave Uncle Ted a tongue-lashing for leaving Andy alone on such a night and said he was as irresponsible as his brother.

Uncle Ted had groaned and pulled his nose in an agony of apology. To Andy he said, "As sure as God is my witness, I'll not allow a drop of the spirits to touch my lips ever again, as long as I'm at Kirriemuir."

Andy didn't believe him, however, and continued to keep a careful eye on him.

One Saturday morning at the end of November he was helping his mother clean up the garden. "Mom," he said, "do you think it would be OK to ask Morgie Wilks to come stay with us for a few days over the Christmas holiday?"

"Sure. I don't see why not. Call him up. But check with Quinn first."

"You don't call him Mr. McAtee any more."

"Andy, there's something I've got to talk to you

about." She straightened up from her basket of weeds and faced him across the row. Her voice was serious. "This might come as a shock to you, but Mr. McAtee has asked me to marry him." She waited for the expected outburst of horror.

"No!" For his mother's benefit he gave a whistle of disbelief. "You don't say!"

She searched his face for signs of sarcasm.

"What did you tell him?"

"That I'd let him have my answer after I'd told you."

"So now you've told me."

She looked worried. "What do you think of the idea?"

He smiled. "If that's what you want, Mom, I think it's a great idea."

"You do!" She couldn't believe it.

"The way you've been looking at one another like lovesick owls, I knew it was sure to come sooner or later. I'm happy for you, Mom."

She took his hands in hers. "Be happy for us all, Andy. We'll be a family again, with a proper home. You like Quinn, don't you?"

"He's OK." Andy shrugged. When he saw his mother's face drop he laughed. "No, I mean I like him. He takes a lot of getting used to, but I'm starting to like him a lot."

His mother smiled happily. "He'll be a good father to you, Andy, wait and see." By now they had walked over to the house. Andy's mother sat on the low brick wall near the door and clasped her hands between the knees of her faded blue jeans. "Oh, Andy, there's such a future for us here at Kirriemuir! Every day is a wonder. Don't you just love it here?"

"I like it."

"Not good enough. Say you love it!"

He laughed, caught up in his mother's enthusiasm. "I love it."

"And we'll get another dog to make us a family of four, and we'll all live at Kirriemuir and live happily ever after." She gave her words a storytelling lilt meant to bring another smile to her son's lips and have him remember how she once read fairytales to him.

He smiled at her. His mother was so happy she was acting like a kid. The little orange flecks in her green eyes shone like gold.

There came a rattle of workboots in the cobbled yard. "It's Quinn," she said happily.

"No, it's Uncle Ted." Andy had been observing his approach.

"You two better drop whatever you're doing," Uncle Ted called as drew near to the house. "Mr. McAtee says for you to head on over to the tractor shed right away. He's got something real important to show you."

"Both of us?" said Andy. He squinted across the yard at the open door of the shed.

"Yep." Uncle Ted pulled the tip of his nose in confirmation.

"What's this 'real important' stuff-and-nonsense, Edward? You know I don't like mysteries. What is it?"

"I ain't supposed to say, Lucy, but . . . " He glanced back at the shed to see if McAtee was watching him. " . . . I'll tell you this much: it's to do with the dog, with McAtee's collie."

"Finder!" said Andy. "What's happened to her?"

But Uncle Ted pressed his lips together in a thin hard line. He'd already said too much.

Andy ran. His mother followed more slowly.

As he ran, he remembered Patch killed under the wheels of the tractor. Was it now Finder's turn for an accident? But no — that wasn't fair. McAtee would never deliberately kill a dog, not unless it was in great pain or was dying. He knew that now. Besides, Finder was a farm dog. She'd never run at a tractor or get caught up in the harvester. He had been wrong to blame McAtee for Patch's death. McAtee was right — Patch was a city dog, just as Andy himself had been a city kid. McAtee's gruff manner had had him fooled. Patch's death was an accident. His mother had known that all along.

So whatever it was that was wrong with Finder wasn't McAtee's fault, of that he now felt certain. He burst in to the shed. McAtee was down at the far end with his back to him. The shed was full of November shadows and the heavy ripe smell of fruit.

"What happened to Finder?" Andy came up behind McAtee and looked down over his wide shoulders at the collie sprawled in a bed of hay. "Is she sick?"

"Nothing the matter with the dog. Come see." He moved so Andy could kneel beside him.

"Pups!" said Andy. "Finder has a litter of pups!" McAtee smiled.

Andy's mother came up behind them. "Pups!" she echoed softly. "How many?"

The tiny pups, no bigger than pork sausages, huddled together blindly at Finder's belly where it was soft and warm. Andy counted them: "Five."

Uncle Ted clattered in and stood smiling down at the nativity scene. "Ain't no dog hereabouts so far as I know," he mused quietly, "so who's the proud father of these here littl'uns, I wonder?" He was grinning like someone who already knew the answer to his own riddle.

McAtee reached out and gently picked up one of the pups. He held it in the palm of his hand. "There's your answer," he said.

Andy and his mother stared at the four sable-and-white pups at their mother's belly. Then they stared at the woolly blue thing in McAtee's hand.

"Blue!" they said together.

McAtee nodded his head. Andy's mother laughed. "That sneaky alien sheepdog!"

"He's yours, boy," said McAtee, "if you want him. Sire's owner takes the pick of the litter, that's usual."

"If I *want* him!" Andy gave a whoop of joy. "You bet I do, Mr. McAtee. Thanks! Thanks a hundred million!" He stopped. "It wouldn't matter, but you're sure he's a he?"

"I'm sure." McAtee's laugh was a rumble in his chest. He glanced up at Andy's mother and raised his eyebrows in a silent question.

She smiled and nodded her head.

McAtee turned to Andy. "And seeing as how you know your mother and I are planning to marry real soon, maybe you ought to start calling me Quinn instead of Mr. McAtee. After all, I'll be your stepfather. Unless you'd prefer Dad or Father or some such?"

"Quinn is fine," said Andy hurriedly, "so long as you stop calling me 'boy.' He reached out his hands. "Can I hold him?"

McAtee passed the pup over. "Careful, boy — Andy. He's only a few hours old. Can't see anything yet."

He cradled the tiny thing in his hands. "I can't believe he's mine, all mine."

McAtee stepped back behind the kneeling boy and took Andy's mother's hand in his.

"I'll call him Blue-Two," said Andy. "Blue for short." He placed the pup carefully back with the others and gently stroked Finder's soft sable coat.

The new mother pushed her nose into the warm hay and closed her eyes contentedly.

"Thanks, Finder," Andy whispered in the collie's ear, "thanks for finding Blue for me."